James Payn

For Cash Only

Vol. 2

James Payn

For Cash Only
Vol. 2

ISBN/EAN: 9783337047436

Printed in Europe, USA, Canada, Australia, Japan

Cover: Foto ©Andreas Hilbeck / pixelio.de

More available books at **www.hansebooks.com**

FOR CASH ONLY

FOR CASH ONLY

A Novel

By JAMES PAYN

AUTHOR OF ' BY PROXY,' ' LOST SIR MASSINGBERD,' ' HIGH SPIRITS,'
' LESS BLACK THAN WE'RE PAINTED,' ' UNDER ONE ROOF,'
ETC.

IN THREE VOLUMES
VOL. II.

London
CHATTO AND WINDUS, PICCADILLY

CONTENTS OF VOL. II.

FOR CASH ONLY.

CHAPTER XVIII.

HALVES.

THERE is a beautiful Eastern poem which describes a mother with her dead child applying to her deity for its resuscitation, and being recommended by way of prescription its being rubbed with mustard-seed, begged from some house into whose doors death had never entered. The mustard-seed was to be got in plenty, but not, of course, under those conditions.

'There is no flock, however watched and tended,
But one dead lamb is there ;
There is no fireside, howe'er defended,
But has one vacant chair.'

And in the case of the aged and infirm the calamity is still more common and to be looked for. But though she knew all that, and had been expecting the stroke to fall for many a day, her father's death for the time quite prostrated Clare. Independent of spirit as she was as regarded her fellow-creatures, she was not one to rebel against the will of God, but resignation was at first impossible to her. She had been, as we know, the very apple of her father's eye, and there had been none to share the love she had reciprocated.

Her affection for Percy was, of course, of another kind; and though her regard for Herbert was very great, it bore no comparison with that she entertained for her parent. So long as the tie, however frail, which had bound the dead man to life existed, she had interested herself in all that interested him, entered into his plans (so much of them at least as he confided to

her), and in all but one thing (a most important exception, however) had conformed
herself to his wishes. And now, when
she had lost him, it almost seemed to her
that she no longer belonged to the great
human family. It was not only that she
was orphaned, but isolated. There was no
loving bosom on which she could fall
and discourse upon him; to Percy especially her lips were sealed, for how could
· she speak of him to one who loved him
not? Herbert, indeed, could have sym-
pathised with her on that topic, and the
knowledge of the fact endeared him to
her; but circumstances had interposed to
prevent her obtaining that solace. What
she wanted was some one faithful friend
of her own sex, and that was denied
her.

The state of her father's health had of late
withdrawn him much from society, as the
fact of his second marriage had formerly
done, and she had made it a rule never to

leave him for any purpose of mere gaiety;
so that though beloved by many of the
poor folks in Stokeville, among whom she
was a constant visitor, Clare had no in-
timate acquaintances among those of her
own rank. Mildred and she had never
been sympathetic, and under present circumstances that young lady's society was
anything but agreeable to her. For the
few days, in short, that followed her father's
decease, Clare felt that the only true companionship left to her was with that irre-
sponsive something above stairs, to which
the inexorable law compelled her to pay
her last adieu.

When that was over she wrote to the
only woman in the world whom she could
call her friend, and who had already
written to her on her bereavement, to
beseech her, for the sake of old times, to
come to Oak Lodge.

This lady was a Miss Darrell, who had
been a pupil-teacher at the same school as

her mother, and had remained her lifelong friend. Subsequently she had started
an educational establishment of her own,
and having met with somewhat exceptional
success, had retired upon her savings.
Clare and she had constantly corre-
sponded, and the elder lady had more
than once been her father's guest, but
she had not been to Stokeville for many
years.

The kind-hearted old lady had answered
in person her young friend's pressing invitation at once; not a day too soon, for Clare
was not only in sorrow, but in trouble.
Before John Lyster was cold in his grave,
there had been a constant babble in the
neighbourhood about the state of his affairs,
some of which perforce had reached Clare's
ears, though far from attentive to any such
things. She had desired to be left alone
a little with her grief, and not to have it
intruded upon by baser topics, but this had
been denied to her.

The very condolements offered had
been in many cases unwelcome to her,
since they were accompanied by vague
allusions to the opportuneness of the
calamity they deplored. 'We all rejoice
to hear that your material interests
will still remain connected with Stokeville. Since it was to be, alas, dear Miss
Lyster, it is a great satisfaction to us to
reflect that it happened when it did,' etc.,
etc. In one instance, from one of her
poorer *protégés*, the allusion was even still
more direct. 'We are thankful to think,
miss, for your sake, that your poor father
died in the very nick of time.'

With a worn and weary air, in which
there was little indeed of curiosity, Clare
had inquired of her cousin to what these
allusions referred. With a delicacy and
forethought that very literally did as much
honour to his heart as his head, Herbert
not only answered her question but went
beyond it. To the outside world the whole

transaction appeared in the light of a lucky
stroke of business ; they knew by this time
that ' old John Lyster' (for being dead he
was already old) by living a few minutes
into the current year had thereby secured
his partnership in the firm for the next
twelve months ; but they did not know what
a difference it had made to those he had left
behind him.   They imagined that they
would have been rich enough in any case ;
but as it was, that they would be million-
aires.   If they had been cognisant of the
dying man's hopes and fears, of his passionate longings to protract existence, the profit
arising from his success would have been
a sufficient explanation of them.   But, as
Herbert well understood, this would not
have been the case with Clare.   To her mind
the struggles and anxieties which she had
witnessed, and of which the secret was now
revealed to her, would have had no adequate
cause ; nay, that her father's mind at such
a time should have been so monopolised

by the acquisition of gain for gain's sake,
would have been a serious moral shock to
her, and gone far to taint an unsullied
memory. It was, therefore, necessary for
him to hint what Mr. Oldcastle had confided to him as his 'suspicions,' but which
to Herbert's ear (besides explaining many
things which of late had puzzled him) conveyed a certainty, viz., that Mr. Lyster's
private estate was far from being what it
was supposed to be. Herbert began by
speaking of it to her as 'far from large,'
and ended with 'indeed, perhaps, next to
nothing,' as though it were intelligence that
required 'breaking;' a piece of tact and tenderness that was, however, thrown away.
Indeed, strange as it may seem to those
whose motto is 'For cash only,' the poorer
he represented her father to have been,
the more grateful was the news to his
listener. For the poorer he had been,
by so much the more explicable became
his eager desire for life, not for its own

sake, but for that of others : instead of self,
it was plain that self-sacrifice had been
actuating him, and that that stubborn resist-
ance of his to his death had been, in fact, an
heroic struggle.

To this view, Dr. Dickson, who looked
in daily as an old friend, gave unconscious
corroboration. In telling her, as he had
previously told Sir Peter, that in his opinion
Mr. Lyster's life had been prolonged by his
own marvellous power of will, he had meant
to point a moral, to show that the depression of mind and body from which she herself was suffering, could be mitigated by
her own act, and to preach the duty of
'making an effort' from her father's example ; and his arguments, although he
mistook the cause of their success, bore fruit
in an increase of cheerfulness in his patient.
It is some consolation, when one has loved
and lost, to know how worthy was the
departed of our regret; and to the sorrowing eyes of Clare the dead man seemed not

only her father, but a hero — almost a
martyr. The lightest word that threw a
shadow of a shade upon his memory was
abhorrent to her, and in this respect the
society of her half-brother was almost intolerable to her. His behaviour, as we have
said, during the latter portion of his father's
illness, had improved, and his habits grown
more domestic or orderly ; nor could it be
said that in the house of mourning he con-
ducted himself with any indecent levity :
but it was now very clear that his late
depression of spirits had not been caused
by filial sorrow, but by anxiety upon his
own account. And what was very characteristic in the young man, he credited his
half-sister with the same feelings, only
overlaid with a thicker tarpaulin of hypocrisy than it was in his nature to assume.
For several days he had restrained himself
from talking on the matter, which, as he
was convinced, lay nearest to both their
hearts ; but on the night before the funeral,

finding himself alone with Clare, he ventured to touch upon it.

'To-morrow, my dear sister,' he said,
'will decide our future positions in life ;
but I am sure it will make no difference in
our mutual relations.'

Clare, deep in sorrowful thoughts,
looked up amazed, as much perhaps at
the unaccustomed elaboration of the young
gentleman's language, which was worthy
of Mr. Roden himself, as of the sentiment
it conveyed.

'Indeed, Gerald, I hope we shall not
only be no worse friends than of yore, but
much better. That you are your father's
son is a tie that has been ever binding to
me, even when you have strained it most ;
and now that he is gone, you are, in a
sense, all of him that is left to me.'

'Just so—his representative,' said Gerald.
'But, as Mr. Oldcastle says, that which
means everything to-day may mean nothing
to-morrow.'

'I don't understand,' said Clare, pressing her hand to her forehead, and looking at him wearily but not unkindly.

'Well, you see, it will depend upon the nature of his will.'

'Oh, I see,' she sighed ; 'you are thinking of his money.   Don't you think that at all events to-night, Gerald, we might speak of him with reference to other subjects, or not at all ?'

'No, Clare.   It distresses me as much as yourself to talk business at such a time, but to-morrow would, in some respects, be too late for discussing the matter.   I wish to assure you that notwithstanding our dear father has made me his heir, as I have reason to believe he has done, I shall take advantage of no legal technicality, but share and share alike with you.'

Clare knew her half-brother pretty well, and excusing and pleading for him as she had often done to others, had been conscious of a weak cause and, to say the least, an 'unsatisfactory client;' but she could not believe that in such a solemn hour Gerald would tell her a deliberate lie. She believed, because he had said it, that her father had made him his heir; and she gave him credit for the resolution he expressed, or rather for the momentary impulse that moved him so to express himself.

'Your offer is a very generous one, Gerald, and gives me as much pleasure from its intention as perhaps anything could give me just now. But my acceptance of it is out of the question. If my father has made you his heir, he has done it for some purpose that seemed good to him, and I hope will prove good for you; and nothing would induce me to be a party to any transaction counter to his wishes. I never wanted dear papa's money, but only his love; and that, thank Heaven, he gave me.'

'Yes, but one can't live on love, Clare,

and far less on the recollection of it. What I want to assure you is that in any event I will take care to see you comfortably provided for. I assure you that makes a great difference, as Percy himself will tell you. He is very fond of you, of course, and all that; but if it turns out that you have nothing to speak of, only a few thousands, if so much, or a small share in the business——'

Clare drew herself up proudly and looked him straight in the face.

Gerald saw that this line of argument was altogether dangerous : it was as though what he had taken for a ford was deep water. It was difficult to retrace his steps, and he began to flounder.

'Of course he will keep his word, and marry you at all events ; but—but—things would not look rosy. Sir Peter, who thinks of nothing but money, would, for one, be sure to object ; and, in short, it might be very unpleasant.'

'I cannot help that, Gerald,' said Clare, in icy tones. 'It may be as you say.' Indeed, it struck her for the moment that her father, in his extreme dislike to Percy, might have left her portionless with the very object of breaking off the marriage. 'If Percy does not love me for my own sake, or even partly for my own sake, it is better that we should not marry. As to Sir Peter, I care nothing for his consent.'

'Quite right,' said Gerald, thankful to have got to land somehow, and glad to have found a topic of agreement. 'Sir Peter is a mercenary old scoundrel; and, as to his daughter, I am sure it's no great feather in your cap that you should have cut *her* out —nasty, purse-proud thing!'

'Cut her out!'

'Well, that's all past and gone; but it's generally believed she used to throw sheep's eyes at Percy. People always said you were worth a dozen of her; but if you were left dowerless and he cried off, of course

Mildred would be pleased—that's only in nature.'

Gerald had drawn his bow at a venture, but, perceiving that the first shot had told, he was ready with a quiverful.

'It is not necessary, I think,' said Clare, 'to discuss Mildred Fibbert's character, nor to retail all the illnatured gossip that may be afloat in Stokeville concerning her.'

She spoke coldly, and her face was fixed and white; but at heart her half-brother's words had affected her even more than he suspected. She had every confidence in her lover, but he had spoken to her of 'ruin' in case his uncle quarrelled with him; and if she was indeed a beggar, or what Sir Peter would consider so, the knight would without doubt, as Gerald said, 'object' to her marriage with his nephew, and if that was broken off—and at the thought of it, Clare, who was but a woman, though a brave one, felt sick at heart—it would certainly be a bitter humiliation to her and a triumph to Mildred.

'I care no more about gossip than you do, my dear Clare,' continued Gerald, with unaccustomed energy : 'what people say goes in at one ear and out at the other ; it is the facts that stick. You and I are now alone in the world—quite alone' (it was Gerald's habit when lying—upon the principle, perhaps, of two negatives making an affirmative—to reiterate the particular falsehood he wished to inculcate), 'and should have all things in common.'

He hesitated, and Clare, only half hearing him, and with her thoughts on other matters, inclined her head.

'Just so; I am so glad that you agree with me,' he went on, quickly. 'Now " all things " of course includes the property ; and I do assure you it would be a great comfort to me, notwithstanding my own reasonable expectations, if you would, as I have proposed, agree to share and share alike. I have a little memorandum in my pocket, if you wouldn't mind putting your name to it along with mine.'

The importunity of his manner aroused her; she looked up suddenly from the depth of her sorrows and forebodings into Gerald's face.

It was the countenance of a lad of only seventeen, but disfigured by a crowd of evil passions, hate feigning love, base expectation struggling with despair, rapacity, greed. She shrank from it as if it had been the Gorgon's.

'I will sign nothing,' she said, with an involuntary shudder ; 'I will talk no more with you to-night.'

'As you please,' he answered, with an ugly look ; 'I meant no offence, I'm sure.'

They sat over the fire, side by side, without speaking for a minute or two. Then Gerald rose with a yawn.

'It is growing late, and to-morrow will be a trying day—a very trying day—for both of us. You should take all the rest you can. Good-night, dear.'

'Good-night.'

She could not bring herself to add the 'dear;' she felt as if the sight of that evil face had been a revelation of the other's nature. It recurred to her again and again in the night—that night of all others, on which she would have thought of other things—and gave to her melancholy dreams a tinge of horror.

CHAPTER XIX.

HOW often it happens that even the average man—one who is neither thief nor scoundrel—goes to his last home without a single genuine mourner ; women as a rule (and it is a good one) do not attend funerals, and it is the women who bewail our loss. Widow and daughter sit at home reading the prayers that are said over the dead, and hearing, in imagination, the earth strewn on the coffin-lid. They will miss us, as our own sex, who have other friends to fall back upon, other things to think about, will never do, and they know it. 'A man's rare tears,' a 'Well,

well ; he was a decent fellow,' and our last duties are paid.

It was so in John Lyster's case ; Herbert Newton alone was moved as the earth closed over his old friend and relative. Sir Peter stood—with his eyes shut—regretfully enough, thinking of that unfortunate five minutes of survival which had so seriously marred the promise of his gains for the whole twelve months. Percy, while taking a much more cheerful view of that particular incident, bethought him with serious face of the state of the deceased's affairs. From all he could gather, though he had no doubt of her inheriting the bulk of his property, there would be very little ready money at Clare's disposal, and he wanted ready money. Mr. Oldcastle, who knew more than anybody about the matter, and yet not much, was full of cogitations on the same subject. Dr. Dickson, more than professionally moved by the sad ceremony, repeated to himself the date upon the coffin-plate, and passed a silent eulogy upon his lost patient's pluck. Mr. Roden, who had been very unwillingly summoned to Stokeville, leaned over the grave, and mournfully shook his head; the snow was on the ground, and he was doubtful whether his feet were not getting wet, in which case a cold was certain, accompanied by a total deprivation of taste. He had been informed by Mr. Oldcastle that he had been made trustee with him and executor, and he was wondering how he could with decency refuse to act.

Gerald outdid the mutes in looking the very picture of woe. He was thinking of how matters would stand with him an hour hence or so, when the contents of the will should have been made known; of the wife he had secretly taken to himself a few months back, and of whom he had already grown weary; and of a certain other matter, small in itself, but the consequences of which might be tremendous and overwhelming. There was, indeed, good cause for his white face and haggard eyes.

And all this time Clare was in her father's room, upon her knees, with thoughts unutterable, and a bruised heart that she almost accused of hardness because it would not break, and suffer her to join him whithersoever he had gone.

Clare did not attend the reading of the will, which took place immediately after the funeral, in the drawing-room of Oak Lodge; and her absence was, perhaps, a fortunate circumstance. There was no 'scene' of any kind, but the expression of Gerald's listening face would probably have frightened her for the second time. That young gentleman must have been misinformed when he had stated to her that he was his father's heir. He had but one-sixth of the property outside the firm, while the remaining five-sixths and the whole of the money in the firm was left to Clare. Wrapped up in the

will, which was the same which Mr. Oldcastle had drawn up for the deceased, was
a letter for Herbert Newton, 'to be destroyed unopened if I live to the first of
January,' and which the lawyer accordingly
put in the fire.   The money for Gerald was
left, of course, in trust.   'It is my express
wish,' the testator added, that no lump sum
be given to my son Gerald, while under
age, by his half sister, nor at any other
time, unless under such conditions as shall
ensure its not being squandered.'

Contingently—that is to say if the expectations of the firm respecting their receipts
for the current year should prove correct—
Clare was thus left a great heiress.   But
what Mr. Lyster had died possessed of,
independently of his share in the firm, could
not at present be ascertained.   There was
a long memorandum of shares and securi-
ties, arranged in the most methodical manner, over which Mr. Oldcastle privately
shook his head, but to which he made

no reference on this occasion. Sir Peter looked as if he would have liked to have asked a question or two, but it was clearly not his business ; while Gerald, who was so nearly concerned, said not a word. Indeed, judged by the ear, the young man had behaved very well under what were undoubtedly trying circumstances ; but his face, especially when that reference to the ' lump sum' was being made, wore a very sinister look. One might have almost fancied it a picture designed by some weird artist, under which he had scrawled ' The Parricide.'

When the company had dispersed Gerald did address a few words to Mr. Oldcastle, who listened to him with considerable commiseration.

' No doubt, my lad, you are disappointed. Whether deservedly or not, your own conscience is the best judge. I am bound to confess, however, when drawing up your father's instructions I myself made no pro-

test.   Your behaviour, you must be aware,
has not inspired confidence.'

' So it seems,' said Gerald bitterly.

' Still, there is nothing in this,' continued
the lawyer, laying his hand upon the will,
' to cause you disquietude for the future.'

' Indeed !   One-sixth of what my father
has left behind him is not a fortune, I suppose ?'

' I am afraid not ; I should say indeed,
though I have not looked into the matter,
far from it.   It may be even a misfortune :
that is, there may be a large deficit.   Your
future will depend upon your good behaviour, which is what, as I conjecture, your
father intended.'

' I don't understand,' said Gerald doggedly.

' Well, if your father had died before the
year was out, I could not have so put it.
In that case you would have had but a pittance at the very best, besides your salary
from the mill.   On the other hand, Clare

would have been no better off, perhaps.'

'You think the residue so small as that?'

'I think it may amount to less than nothing. But even supposing it had amounted
to a few thousands—yes' (this in reply to a
stifled execration, which the lawyer charit-
ably set down as a groan); 'the fact is, your
father's speculations have been most unfortunate. He took his own way; he was never
a man to ask advice,' he continued, almost
in soliloquy, 'and generally, I must say,
most judicious. It was the desperate effort
to recoup himself, no doubt; otherwise, I
can't account for it.'

'You are speaking of the residue,' said
Gerald hoarsely.

'To be sure. I was about to observe
that the interest of five-sixths of it would
not, in any case, have exceeded your own
income. So far, in short, Clare and yourself were placed on the same footing.'

'What!' hissed the other between his

teeth, ' with all the money in the business left to her absolutely ?'

' The money was her mother's, not *your* mother's, Gerald. You had no sort of claim to it. Excuse me, but your manner compels me to be frank.'

' No doubt—thank you,' answered the other, moistening his lips with his tongue. 'Notwithstanding all this frankness, your meaning as to my not being " disquieted," and the advantage of my being on my "good behaviour," is not clear to me.'

' Well, I mean that Clare has it in her power to help you, and I am sure that she will do so to any reasonable extent.'

' But the will forbids that.'

' Only as to a lump sum. There I think your father was quite right. What can a boy like you want with a lump sum ? I shall advise your sister to allow you a certain income.'

' How much ?'

' Well, really, Gerald, that is a matter

for consideration. At present your expenses can hardly be very great. You will continue to live here, of course. What can you want with money?'

'I do want it,' was the curt reply.

'Well, well, we will see about all that. Clare is not one to close her purse-strings against anyone.'

'And when Clare is married am I to be dependent upon that infernal Percy?'

'Hush, hush! Pray restrain yourself. No; I think that would be very improper. I shall do my best to persuade Clare to keep her money in her own hands.'

'She is in love with him, and a fool besides. She will give it him all.'

'No, sir. Your sister is not a fool. Moreover, she has a sense of filial duty,' answered the lawyer sternly. 'She will, I know, be guided by her father's wishes in this matter, which he expressed to me very precisely.'

'Why didn't he tie the money up?' asked

Gerald passionately. 'He knew how to do it, it seems.'

'You are an ungrateful son, sir, and your passion blinds you,' answered the lawyer coldly. 'It ought to be sufficient for you to know that your father had his reasons. One of them, moreover, was, I am well convinced, that Clare should be at liberty to act towards you with liberality.'

'What does all that come to?' returned the other contemptuously; 'put it in figures.'

'That is impossible just now. The amount will depend upon your needs, but still more upon your deserts. That is the point, which, as your father's friend, and one who will be yours if you will let him, I wish to impress upon you.'

'You mean that I am to be in leading-strings all my life?'

'At all events before you are out of them you must convince us—that is, your trustees and your sister—that you are competent to take care of yourself.'

Mr. Oldcastle turned away as though he had nothing more to say, and sat down at the dead man's desk. He opened it with a key he produced from his own pocket.

'I wish to say,' said Gerald, in a subdued and humble tone, 'that if I can be of any use to you in arranging those papers, I shall be glad to help you. My father employed me of late in all his smaller business affairs. The petty cash, and the cheques drawn on his private account, and so on.'

'Very good. I will apply to you in case anything requires an explanation. In the meantime say nothing of what I have told you as respects your late father's private estate. Things may turn out better than I expect, and on the other hand much worse. In either case it will make little difference to you.'

'You mean that the anticipated profits of the firm this year are so large that this other matter is a mere fleabite.'

'I meant nothing of the kind, sir. The profits of the firm, whatever they may be, will not be yours. I only wished to impress upon you once again that your prospects will depend upon your own conduct. I have nothing to add to that.'

Gerald felt that he had not conciliated the lawyer, and had done himself more harm than good. But conciliation is not easy to us when the chief desire of our minds is to possess a hatchet and the opportunity of terminating with it the lives of one's immediate friends and relatives. Never, he thought, in the history of the world had anyone been so infamously treated as he had been. The idea of his future depending upon his good behaviour was especially abhorrent to him, and indeed seemed almost cynical—like a bequest to a man with a wooden leg, which should be made contingent upon his distinguishing himself in pedestrianism. That a chit of a girl like Clare should hold the purse-strings of his supplies was the circum-stance that galled him most of all. How much more in accordance with the fitness of things it would have been to have made him the almoner and her the recipient. And this terrible disinheritance, although his last and crowning misfortune, was not the worst thing that could befall him. He was environed on every hand by troubles which were not the less hateful because they were of his own making. Besides having to cringe to Clare, and if possible to cajole her, it was necessary for him in other matters to wear a mask of serenity: and, though his very soul was bursting with chagrin and impatience, to move with caution and pick his way.

As he was about to mount the stairs to Clare's boudoir (for the task of conciliation could not be begun too soon) he saw Percy

coming out of it. He marked him close
the door and stand for a moment outside
with frowning face. The interview he
rightly conjectured (like his own with Mr.
Oldcastle) had been an unsatisfactory one,
and it had cost him something to play his
part in it. He was waiting, no doubt, for
the thunder-cloud to clear from his brow,
and the smile to come back, with which it
was his custom to meet his fellow-creatures
when it was worth his while to do so.
Was it possible that after all that had
come and gone Clare had refused him?
To Gerald such an event would have been
indeed welcome; it was most desirable
that she should have her mind free from
thoughts of love and fixed on duty—the
duty of providing for her nearest relative.
But that seemed too great a piece of luck
to be true. It was clear, however, that
there was a rift in the lute of love; its
harmony had received some check, and
apparently a rude one.

Percy descended step by step with downcast eyes, and so rapt in thought that he did not see the other till he was close upon him.

'What the deuce are you grinning at?' he then exclaimed imperiously.

'Grinning! I was only looking at you! A cat may look at a king, and grin too, for that matter.'

' I am glad you are in such good spirits,' replied Percy, with a sneer. 'I should have hardly expected it.'

The hostile character of these remarks was immensely heightened by their being uttered on both sides in a subdued tone, necessitated by the circumstances of the case. Each of the antagonists was careful not to make a disturbance in the house of mourning. Percy's last innuendo, referring, as Gerald well understood, to the contents of his father's will, was, however, almost insupportable to him. It was with difficulty he restrained himself from an outburst; as it was, he glared at the other in silent fury.

'After all,' continued Percy, who, having found an object, was evidently giving rein to the passion which he had hitherto been obliged to suppress, 'it is not as if you wanted money. A lad like you, without incumbrance—a gay young bachelor at most—can afford to smile at being disinherited.'

'That's true,' said Gerald slowly. 'If I had really expensive tastes, such as keeping racehorses for example, the thing would be more serious.'

'Racehorses? Who keeps racehorses?' answered Percy. His tone was indifferent, and even contemptuous; but to one who observed him narrowly (and for once Gerald's eyes gazed point-blank upon his interlocutor), it could be seen that he turned a little pale, and that his moustache was twitching uneasily.

'Oh, I don't know; let us say, for example, Jennings.'

'To be sure,' said Percy with a faint smile, and in a voice that was also faint.

'Well, he would sometimes want money, I should think. And as to disinheritance, why that is a thing that might happen to anybody.'

'Quite true, Gerald. I was wrong, however, to make light of it in your case. The fact is I have been put out, and scarcely knew what I said. Forgive me.'

This was a point so very opportune for the utterance of his favourite interjection that Gerald could not resist it. Indeed, so far from rejecting it he gave it full stress and significance, so that it sounded like the malignant snarl of a dog.

'Yah.'

'Come, don't be sulky,' said the other quietly. 'I mean you no harm, but quite the contrary. You are not perhaps in such a hole as you think; and if you are, I

may be able to help you out of it. If
there's anything pressing——'

'I want twenty pounds,' interrupted
Gerald.

'Twenty pounds,' repeated Percy. His
face had become very quiet and thoughtful; he appeared to be reflecting as to
whether he had the money about him, for
he felt in his breast-pocket for his notebook. But the real question he was
putting to himself was a far more important one. 'If I suffer this horse-leech
to draw blood once, will he cling to me
for ever?' 'Yes,' he said, drawing four
bank-notes from a largish roll of them, 'I
will lend you twenty pounds with pleasure;
and I dare say we shall not quarrel about
the repayment.'

'I dare say not,' sneered Gerald; 'and
as to helping me in a general way—I mean
as to the allowance that is to be made to
me by Clare and so forth—I dare say I
may look to you for that also.'

'My influence will certainly be exerted in your behalf.'

'That sounds very pretty, but I am not going to be put off with a pittance. If that is all Clare does for me it must be made up to me by somebody else; do you understand?'

'Make your mind quite easy upon that subject, Gerald.'

Percy nodded assuringly as he let himself out at the front door, and walked down the gravel-sweep swinging his cane. Gerald gazed after him with grim admiration.

'What a fellow he is to carry a thing off! He is the best and greatest liar alive, I do believe. One would think that that twenty pounds was all he would have to pay to yours truly. But he knows as well as I do that it's only the beginning of our little running account. Sam Chigwell, you scoundrel, I owe you a good turn for this; not that you meant it however, for you would never have let the cat out of the bag if you hadn't been drunk. And I didn't know about it myself for certain till I saw the fellow's face twitch. That's a hint old Dickson gave me which I have not forgotten. A man's mouth will often tell the truth when his tongue lies. That "let us say, for example, Jennings," was a bold stroke of mine. But what a fool I was to say twenty instead of fifty! To think that some fellows should go about with rolls of notes when a man like me is in want of a sovereign. It's disgusting. However, I shall not want for sovereigns now—thanks to Jennings.'

CHAPTER XX.

E VERYBODY says that it is better
to be good than to be clever, though
very few people believe it. A judge the
other day, indeed, took off half the punishment he should have inflicted upon a very
cruel murderer, because he was informed
that the man was 'by disposition dull and
slow;' but that was an exceptional case
arising probably out of his lordship's fellow-
feeling with the prisoner. As a rule, it is
considered that dull people don't 'get on,'
while clever ones do. I have, however,
my doubts upon this subject. The clever
ones climb the ladder of success in life

with great rapidity, but often as not lose
their footing (through slipperiness), and
back they tumble heels over head ; or they
reach the very top even, and then, like
vaulting ambition, fall on the other side.
Percy Fibbert, for example, was perhaps
the cleverest young fellow in Stokeville ;
but his position just now, as one may guess,
was far from enviable. Gerald Lyster, too,
had lots of cleverness, though of the kind
that is called 'cunning ;' and yet, as we
have seen, he had his apprehensions. For
the moment, indeed, it seemed that things
were going better with him, and that in
hitting on a certain blot in the affairs of the
suave and smiling Percy, he had, as it were,
'struck oil.' This, however, was but an
oasis in his desert of troubles. If he had
been a wise man, or even a dull one, he
would have let well alone for awhile ; but
being so astute, he thought that no time
should be lost in paying his court to his
father's daughter and heiress, especially

now he had won her lover over to his side.

So he went up to Clare's room, and, knocking with all the sympathy that could be expressed by the knuckles, was admitted. She was standing by the window with her back to him, and did not turn to meet him for a second or two.

'Blubbing,' said Gerald to himself.

And, indeed, Clare was shedding very bitter tears. Since the death of her father she had been conscious of a barrier, or rather, for it was very thin and vague, we will say a film of obstruction between Percy and herself. She could not forget that her father had not loved him, and she suspected that that antagonistic feeling was at least reciprocated. It seemed just now almost a sort of disloyalty to the dead man's memory to encourage Percy's attentions, and in the late interview she was conscious of having behaved with what he might well consider cruelty. He had not

said so, but on the contrary, which aggravated her remorse, had behaved with ad-
mirable self-control and gentleness.   He
had recognised where the difficulty lay at
once, and had addressed himself to remedy it.

He had described to her, in his pic-
turesque way, the circumstances of the
funeral.   How many of the shops had
been shut in Stokeville (a circumstance
that had escaped the observation of the
other mourners, no doubt from the pre-
occupation of their minds with grief), and
how everyone had testified by their manner
the sense of a loss to the community.
Then he had painted, without exaggera-
tion, his own feelings, or rather what he
imagined she had conceived them to be.
How the knowledge that the dead man
had not understood him was a bitter pang
to him, now that the time had passed for
such understanding ; though on his part
there had been, he was glad to feel, at

least the highest respect and reverence. Indeed, of late (this he put very carefully), he had ventured to hope that Mr. Lyster himself had looked upon him with less unfavourable eyes.

Never perhaps had Percy Fibbert shown himself so clever ; and yet to the ears of loving regret all this had a false ring in it. Clare involuntarily compared it with the few words her cousin Herbert had whispered to her, hand clasped in hand, when he took leave of her, five minutes before, and the lines of contrast had stood out with painful distinctness.

And yet she loved this man with all her heart.

We call 'marvellous' the love that is instinctive, as that of a mother for her child. But how much more marvellous is that which is no instinct, but infatuation, the love of a pure girl for an unworthy object. Clare had cast herself for a moment upon Percy's breast and returned his kisses, for was he not her betrothed and all she had to look to in the future ? But even of that she had almost repented as of an act of treason. And when, on the other hand, he proffered his caresses, and she had avoided them, she felt that she was cruel and unkind. Percy did not put it quite in that way himself, but he thought himself very badly treated. He had no 'patience' with the grief that interfered with his tender affections ; thought it ' infernal rubbish,' and that more than enough had been already sacrificed on the altar of filial sentiment. The provisions of the dead man's will had been satisfactory to him ; but he had looked for nothing less, while he had a strong conviction that his uncle would look for something more. If Mr. Lyster's property, apart from what he had in the mill, should prove to be nothing, or even, as was quite possible, a minus quantity, Sir Peter would be far from satisfied. It was expedient on that account that matters should be arranged for his marriage as speedily as possible ; and still more expedient, inasmuch as a jealous woman, to whom he had not behaved fairly, was bent on putting every obstacle in the way. This last fact, it was true, was his trump-card with Clare, and in an indirect way he continued to play it. But to his bitter disappointment it had not the same effect as on the previous occasion. Sir Peter, and even Mildred, might do their worst, said Clare (or as much as said), but for the present she for her part could not think of marriage; and it was plain that at that time it distressed and pained her to speak about it.

No wonder then that Mr. Percy Fibbert with so many irons in the fire, but thus compelled to inactivity and suspense, should have resented it, and, though he left the boudoir of his lady-love with the gravest and tenderest of smiles, should have stood outside with a frown

on his face (as an angry cat waits for her
tail to go down before she can pass under
some grating) for his rage to subside
before he showed himself to society.

From first to last, however, the astute
Percy had never said one word about
Clare's money.

Now Gerald, though, as we have said,
astute in his way, was quite unable to
steer clear of that important topic: he
took it for granted that both Herbert and
Percy had been full of it; and his first
words on entering his sister's room were:

'Well, Clare, I congratulate you—most
heartily congratulate you.'

She turned from the window with astonishment on her pale and tearful face.

'Congratulate me, Gerald ?'

She scarcely thought she could have
heard aright; he must surely have meant
condolence.

'Well, yes, dear; of course, though you
expected it—or at least we all did.'   It

was bad for Gerald as an habitual liar that
he had a very short memory. 'But I am
so glad that your hopes, and, indeed, my
hopes, are confirmed.'

For the moment she really thought that
this unhappy boy, instead of having all his
wits about him, and the steadiest possible
eye to the main chance, was in liquor.

'I mean, of course,' he added very
cheerfully, for it suddenly struck him that
he might after all be the first bearer of the
good tidings to her, 'I mean that my
father has made you his heiress.'

Luckily for Gerald the material significance of this information, and conse-
quently the motive that prompted it, was
not the first thing that struck Clare; the
news was to her only a fresh 'proof of
the dead man's love, and it utterly over-
came her.

'Don't cry, dear Clare, don't cry; be
sure I am not here to reproach my father.'

'Reproach him, Gerald?' If a glass

of water had been flung in her face, as
Gerald afterwards observed, it could not
have brought her more speedily to herself.
'Why should you reproach him?'

'Of course not, there is no sort of reason
why; and though, as I told you, I was led
to imagine that matters would have been
very differently arranged, I am not at all
jealous—though perhaps just a little disappointed. I have not behaved as I ought
to have done, I know; I did give him reason to distrust me—but, but——' And
Gerald took out his handkerchief and
covered his face.

'My poor Gerald!' said Clare kindly,
with her hand upon his shoulder; 'it was
not distrust, I am sure, but only that he
thought you improvident, and—and—perhaps a little reckless. If he has left what
he had to me, he did so knowing well that
I should see your interests were looked
after.'

'That is just what I told Mr. Oldcastle,'

exclaimed Gerald triumphantly. ' " My
father knew," said I, " that Clare would
never let me be the sufferer. He had such
confidence in her sense of right." '

' I hope so, dear Gerald,' said Clare
humbly.

' And Percy,' continued Gerald, in the
tone of one who makes a candid admission,
' though he has not always shown himself
friendly to me, I must say Percy says the
same. When he talks to you about it, Clare,
if he has not already done so, I am sure you
will find that he takes my side—the side of
justice. That I should be left penniless
and you an heiress would, he allows, be
very hard, if it were not, as Mr. Oldcastle
would say, for the intention of the testator.
The mere words of the will are nothing
when we know what he really meant. I
do not ask, of course, that we should share
and share alike, as we should have done if
things had been the other way ; but some
suitable arrangement — something of the

same kind—Percy thinks should be entered into for my benefit.'

'I think you may trust me,' said Clare, faintly smiling. 'I don't want even Percy to advise me as to right or wrong.'

'No, nor Herbert either,' said Gerald quickly, for next to making sure of our friends, it is as well to provide against our enemies. 'Herbert has always done his best to worm himself into my father's good graces, and set him against me.'

'Oh, Gerald, Gerald! don't say that; Herbert is justice itself.'

'Well, you'll see. He'll be the very man to oppose my getting my rights. It was he, I know, who suggested that I should not have a lump sum. That's down in the will.'

'But, my dear Gerald, what can a boy like you want at present with a lump sum, which I suppose means a large sum of ready money. If you have any debts, of course they shall be paid.'

There was a moment when, taking note
of Clare's gentle looks and the tender clasp
of her hand in his, he had a mind to tell
her all. How he had clandestinely con-
tracted a disgraceful marriage ; how something was on its way towards life which
would be a lifelong burden to him ; how
he had lost money, as well as spent it,
which was not his own. But his habitual
cunning restrained him.

'Well, of course I have debts,' he said
doggedly. ' I have expenses, too, as
every young fellow has : as a fellow, I
mean, in my position'—for he saw he was
making a bad impression—' has a right to
have.'

' I will consult with Mr. Oldcastle,
Gerald,' said Clare earnestly, 'and everything shall be managed for the best.
Pray, pray believe that I have nothing
but your good, the good of my dear
father's son, at heart.'

' I had rather you consulted with Percy,

for he's a young fellow himself, and knows. Mr. Oldcastle is an old fogy, and a skin-flint beside. He would suggest, perhaps, three hundred a year.'

In Clare's eyes three hundred a year for a young gentleman who was hardly nineteen, and lived at home, seemed a very sufficient allowance; but she only observed, with a sigh: 'All that shall be seen to, Gerald; but I must take the advice of wiser heads than mine.'

'Well, Percy, of course, would be your natural adviser. I am sure I am quite willing to leave everything to his good feeling and sense of justice.'

Clare thought it strange that Gerald should exhibit this confidence in Percy, between whom and himself, as he had often said, 'there was no love lost;' and it also occurred to her that Mr. Oldcastle, as much the older man, and her father's friend and professional adviser, was the more proper person to consult on such a matter. But as she perceived it would annoy Gerald to say so, she only bowed her head. A sense that she was somehow placed in antagonism to Gerald, or rather that he conceived her to be so, oppressed her and begat a sense of embarrassment. It was literally a relief to her—such as is hailed by a besieged garrison—that her maid now entered the room with 'Mr. Oldcastle's compliments, and if convenient he would come up upstairs and have a few words with her.'

'Now,' said Gerald, with great earnestness, 'you be firm, Clare. The lawyers always go by the letter and not by the spirit ; you mustn't let him breed bad blood between us.'

'Bad blood !'

'I mean, being a lawyer, nothing would probably please him more than that we two should quarrel, which, living as we do under the same roof, would be to the last degree unpleasant.'

The tone as well as the words were menacing, and under other circumstances would have brought the fire of defiance into Clare's eyes. She was not a girl to be coerced into anything ; but on the present occasion she only answered gently :

' It takes two to make a quarrel, Gerald,' and kissed him as he left the room.

Neither the kiss nor the assurance, however, were warmly received. She felt that there were troubles coming of a different sort from those which had hitherto befallen her, and in addition to them. It had been her earnest wish, and even her prayer, that for the future Gerald and she should live as sister and brother ought to do ; but she could not help feeling that it would be very difficult to get on with him. Percy, too, she could not conceal from herself, was far from pleased with her. In a word, she felt not only forlorn and bereaved but isolated.

Thank Heaven, good little Miss Darrell was coming to-morrow.

CHAPTER XXI

MISS ANNIE DARRELL (com-
monly called Nannie by her inti-
mate friends) was a little lady of fifty or
thereabouts, who, thanks to early troubles
and later cares, looked in some respects a
hundred. Her face was deeply lined, her
hair was white as snow, and she had only
a few ounces of flesh on her bones impar-
tially distributed. But her manner was
cheerful and even airy, her eyes bright and
birdlike, and her heart was young. I
should rather say it was rejuvenescent, for
a sort of Indian summer (except that it
was to last) had befallen it. As a pupil

teacher she had tasted very few of the de-
lights of youth—her friendship with Clare's
mother had been the one bright feature of
that dreary existence ; as a governess she
had had a still harder time of it ; and as a
schoolmistress who never shirked her duty
she had been worn, as she herself expressed
it, to fiddle-strings. But competence and
leisure had come at last to her ; and—what,
alas, seldom happens—not too late. Unlike
the birds, she sang in the winter instead of
the spring. Her experience was, for one
of her sex, large and varied ; life had no
longer any illusions for her (indeed, poor
soul, it never had had any), but she found
it enjoyable. Though her face was wrinkled,
it had the delicate complexion of a child,
which, combined with the fragility of her
form and the diminutiveness of her stature,
gave her the look of a figure in Dresden
china.

‘ How good of you to come !’ whispered
Clare, after a long embrace.

' Good of me ! It is the sort of good-
ness most easily practised, the doing what
one likes best. What could be so pleasant
to me as to come to you ? Only, if you
cry I shall go away· again. You know I
never could stand tears.'

She had seen a good deal of them in
her time, nevertheless ; and if she herself,
thanks to the necessity of self-control, had
shed but few, it was not because she had
not had plenty to cry about.

' I cannot help it, Nannie. I was thinking of the last time you were here.'

'When your dear papa was alive. I
understand all that. Do you think, however, he would wish you to weep like that?
That is surely the great point now—how
you can best fulfil his wishes.'

' It is indeed,' sighed Clare, thinking of
many things—of what Mr. Oldcastle had
impressed upon her with respect to Gerald,
of what Gerald himself had said to her, and
chiefly of her lover.

Miss Darrell at once understood that there was a difficulty somewhere, and shifted her ground.

'It is easy to see from your eyes, my poor darling, that your debt of sorrow has been overpaid. Yet your father was a good man.'

'The best of men,' answered Clare fervently.

'Then it is certain he is in heaven.' She was about to add, 'with your sainted mother;' but the remembrance of his second marriage, suggesting a plurality of sainted wives, restrained her. 'And if in heaven, why should you weep? Such behaviour is not only illogical, for it is impossible you can grudge him his eternal happiness, but unfits you for your earthly duties. How can you consider what is best to be done for others—which is what we are given brains for—when your thoughts are fixed upon one for whom you can do nothing; except, of course, carrying out his wishes?'

' But that is the difficulty, Nannie.'

' Tears, however, will only render you less fit to cope with it.'

There was a touch of the schoolmistress in her tone, which was not inopportune. Clare was just now not only in need of a counsellor, but even to some extent of a dictator.

Before an hour had passed, Miss Darrell was in full possession of the circumstances in which her young friend was placed as regarded Gerald ; and had learnt more perhaps than Clare was aware of, or had intended she should, of her relations with Percy.

' I must look at things for a little with my own eyes,' was the old lady's con- clusion, 'before giving you any definite opinion. But I think you may trust to me, at all events as to business matters.'

If Miss Darrell had a weakness it was the conviction that she was a 'woman of business ;' and it must be allowed that she had some cause for it. As a general rule, I have noticed that the ladies who have acquired this reputation derive it from their lawyers, and that it is conferred on account of the number of letters the said clients write to them, each of which demands a reply—price six and eightpence. Miss Darrell had had little or nothing to do with lawyers; but she had a very accurate knowledge of finance and a consciousness of the value of money, which, to persons of sentiment, would perhaps have seemed incompatible with a generous and simple nature. She would have given the very shawl off her back in the bitterest of winter weather to anyone she loved, had such a sacrifice been required ; but she understood the comfort of clothing, and specially the exceeding discomfort arising from its insufficiency. Her sense of the evils of poverty, quickened by long experience, was in no way dulled by her present prosperity ; and, curiously enough,

it indirectly led her to be Gerald's apologist.
Clare had told her—not in the way of complaint of him, but in explanation of that
want of sympathy with her half-brother of
which she had accused herself, and deplored—how he had come on the very day
of her father's funeral to congratulate her
upon being his heiress.

'It seemed to me so sadly ill-timed,' she
said, 'and altogether unsuitable, that I am
afraid it rather set me against him.'

'Then I don't think it should have done
so,' said the old lady bluntly. 'It is a
matter of very great congratulation that
you are left independent of all money cares.
Every other kind of trouble is healed by
time, but those endure for ever. It is only
those who have not felt it who underrate
the pinch of poverty. When sorrow such
as yours overtakes us, it seems for the
time that nothing else is worth thinking
about; but if narrow or insufficient means
accompany it, we have soon to think of

how to make them go as far as possible,
and farther—to stretch what is not elastic.
Our sorrow, which seemed something
divine and eternal, is then quenched in
sordid cares ; but it is a very miserable
way of getting rid of it.   Dear Clare,' continued the old woman, speaking with
energy, ' I had once a free and independent spirit like yourself.   Thank Heaven,
it has been restored to me; but I shall
never forget what it cost me, and how I
lost it.   The shifts I have been put to, the
wretched scrapings and hoardings, the
adding of not house to house and field to
field, but of shilling to shilling — these
things, not to mention the necessity of
holding one's hand when Pity cries " Give,
give," are not easily forgotten.   But, bitterest of all, and the remembrance of which
can never fade, are the slights and con-
tumelies that Poverty compels us to submit to ; the hypocrisies it forces upon us ;
the bated breath, when we should speak

out ; the bended knee, when we should stand upright ; the——' She stopped suddenly, quivering with emotion. ' No matter, dear; all that is past and gone. Where were we ? Talking of Gerald, true. Well, I think he was quite right to congratulate you.'

' I have forgiven him, I am sure. Indeed, your words have put his own in quite a different light. It was the inopportuneness of the time, I think, that struck me. Percy, for example, never dreamt of alluding to money matters.'

' Indeed !' The tone of this remark was what wine merchants term ' extra dry.' ' I suppose it is the privilege of engaged young ladies to know what their lovers dream about.'

' I mean,' said Clare, with a quick flush, ' that Percy has too much good taste and delicacy of mind to have thought of such things at such a time, much less to have talked about them.'

'And Herbert ?'

'And of course Herbert, too. Indeed, at no time does Herbert much concern himself with pecuniary matters. He is consideration and kindness itself, and there is no one—no one—of whom dear papa had a higher opinion.'

'He always gave me the impression of being a very sensible young man,' said Miss Darrell quietly. 'Though he takes nothing under your father's will, it seems, this continuation of partnership with Sir Peter must be of great advantage to him, since he has money in the business.'

'I suppose so ; I'm sure I hope so.'

'But surely you must know. I understood that the year's profits would be enormous.'

'So it is expected; but Mr. Oldcastle took great pains to point out to me that that was but a contingency. I am afraid I did not give him my whole attention, but he hinted that things might possibly go the other way.'

'You mean that the firm might have losses instead of gains, for which your father's estate would be responsible.'

'Yes; and in that case, as I understood him, there would be very little left for poor Gerald to quarrel about.'

'Then there can be nothing but what is *in* the business—no savings?' suggested Miss Darrell thoughtfully.

'I suppose not, at all events very little, and Mr. Oldcastle even spoke of a deficit. There may be liabilities : he said something about an unlimited company.'

'But, my darling, that is most important,' put in the lady earnestly; 'it may mean ruin.'

'You had better talk to Mr. Oldcastle yourself,' said Clare wearily. 'Oh dear, oh dear, this money—it has set Gerald against me already, you see !

'Yes, it's the root of all evil,' assented

the old lady ; ' but there's one thing worse, my dear, than money—and that is, the want of it. How's Sir Peter ?'

' I believe he is as well as usual,' said Clare coldly.

' Ah, so I should suppose, and in his usual spirits ! I should think he was a man who could bear to lose his friends with a great deal of philosophy.'

' I don't think Sir Peter was ever a friend of papa's, though he was his partner.'

' Indeed ! That is what seems to me a risk in partnership that is not duly considered. If there is a common bond of sympathy, well and good ; indeed, nothing could be more pleasant : but if the bond is only one of interest, it must become very irksome. It is almost as great a lottery as marriage.'

' You don't fall in love with your partner, however, before entering with him into business,' said Clare, smiling—for the first time for many a day—at the old lady's seriousness.

'No, you do that with your eyes open, which is so far an advantage. I am not speaking of your case, my dear, of course : you have known Percy Fibbert all his life ; it is not a matter of love at first sight— taking a house to live in all your life, as it were, without inquiries, just because it looks well from the railroad.'

'But I did love Percy at first sight,' smiled Clare. 'You will forgive me, my dear Nannie, for saying that this is one of the few things you don't understand.'

'No doubt, my dear,' answered the old lady simply. 'It's a mystery to spinsters. I have never loved anybody till I felt, so to speak, justified in so doing. I like to have something to go upon. Love seems to me like ice, and one ought to try whether it will bear or not before one ventures.'

Clare laughed again, and this time quite merrily.

'Love is not at all like ice, I do assure you, Nannie.'

'By-the-bye, talking of ice,' said the old lady, 'how is your friend Mildred?'

Clare's face grew very grave. 'She is quite well, I believe; I have not seen much of her lately.'

'Ah, she is not one, I should imagine, who agrees with Solomon that it is better to come to the house of mourning than to that of feasting!'

'I do not say that she has been inattentive, but the fact is we are not very sympathetic.'

'You don't like the same things, or the same people.'

Clare felt the colour glowing in her cheeks, though she would have given worlds to hide it from the other's scrutinising glance.

'We have not the same tastes in any

way,' she answered quietly, 'and I don't think Mildred likes *me*.'

' That is unfortunate, since you are going to marry into the family.'

' Yes, it is so ; one has misfortunes, you see,' she added with a ghost of a smile, ' even though one is an heiress.'

The old lady nodded, and went on with her needlework. (She was always armed with a needle and thread, being constitutionally unable to sit idle for five minutes.) Then the conversation grew more desultory, and she refrained from asking any more questions. She had already possessed herself generally of the map of the country with respect to her young friend's affairs. The by-paths, she flattered herself, she should presently discover for herself.

CHAPTER XXII.

THOUGH Percy Fibbert's last inter-view with Clare had not been wholly satisfactory, his conduct had betrayed no sign of it; his temper, to say the truth, was not of the best, and when once let loose was one of the worst, but he had great control over it. You would never have guessed, to see him in the presence of his betrothed, with that smiling air of his, and only an occasional sigh to show her how cruelly she was treating him, what a volcano of impatience was raging within him. How he despised all that affectation of affection and regret which seemed to find relief in procrastination, and was only one degree less contemptible in his eyes than prudery itself.

Perhaps if he could have told her all, Clare would have named some reasonably early date for their union, but all he dared not tell her ; and mere passionate pleading was not only of no avail in her case, but might defeat its object. He suspected, indeed, what was the fact, that any importunity would have quickened the sense of remorse she entertained in acting counter to the wishes of her father, notwithstanding that consent had been wrung from him. Every week's delay would, he knew, give Mildred hopes of his marriage being broken off, and thus make matters more unpleasant in the end, while it would give opportunity for examination into the state of Mr. Lyster's affairs, which he conjectured were anything but prosperous, a disclosure which would once more place Sir Peter in opposition. It was creditable, therefore, to Percy's self-

restraint that he came daily to Oak Lodge
to play the part of a sympathising friend
rather than that of a lover. He had, however, another reason for his visits, that of
keeping up an intimacy with Mr. Oldcastle,
who was now constantly at the house on business, and who, in spite of Gerald's voluntary
offer of assistance, was much less confidential with him than with Percy. Clare's
coldness whetted his passion, or some of
the lawyer's revelations might have cooled
it, for the young man had as keen an eye
to the main chance as his uncle, though he
pursued it under other conditions. He
liked risk—that is, the gambler's " perfect
certainties "—for its own sake ; and when
he had once promised anything (to himself),
was most honourably resolute to keep his
word. Thus it happened that when Mr.
Oldcastle pointed out that Mr. Lyster's
affairs were not only bad in themselves, but
were involved in certain, or rather uncer-
tain, contingencies, Percy received the in-

formation with considerable philosophy. If an investment was in an unlimited company, then it must be got out of it; if a security was shaky, it must be disposed of for what it would fetch. Advice it was easier to offer than to put into effect. At the same time, Mr. Oldcastle felt that it was good advice, and, knowing that Percy was fully aware of the danger to which the estate was exposed, became more favourably disposed towards the young man for making light of it. They both agreed that the matter should be kept as long as possible a secret, and, as always happens, grew more familiar and confidential from their common possession of it.

One morning, as Percy was leaving the house, the lawyer called him into the study.

'Look here,' he said; 'I have been going into these things,' pointing to a little heap of papers labelled 'Personal Expenses.' 'They are of little consequence, as compared with

other matters; but what do you think of
this ?'

It was one of Mr. Lyster's cheques payable to ' self or bearer,' and crossed as usual,
for £25.

' I see nothing peculiar in it,' said Percy;
' that is his signature, if you mean that.'

' No doubt; but look on the other side.
What do you think of the endorsement ?'

' Samuel Chigwell ! That's odd, certainly.'

Mr. Samuel Chigwell, or Sam Chigwell,
as he was more generally called, was a
cousin of Mr. Lyster's second wife, and the
most disreputable member of what, at best,
was not a very respectable family. He had
some little property of his own, supposed
to have been acquired in the lower walks
of sporting life, such as dog-fighting and
pigeon-shooting, and which had placed him
in the enjoyment of a banker's account.
The late Mrs. Lyster's relatives had never
found her husband the milch cow which

their hopes had pictured him : to herself,
for the short time she had been with him,
he had been liberality itself; and he had
assisted to some extent her immediate
relatives.   But she had not importuned
him in that way, nor had he felt ashamed
of their poverty.   In Stokeville it was so
common for one member of a family to
become suddenly possessed of wealth that
there was no public sense of incongruity ;
and as to the outlying members of the
Chigwell race, Mr. Lyster had seldom
been brought into contact with them.
Least of all had he been acquainted with
Sam, who, indeed, except by hearsay, was
unknown to all respectable people.   It was
no wonder, therefore, that on seeing Mr.
Lyster's cheque with Sam's endorsement
Mr. Percy Fibbert should have exclaimed,
' That's odd, certainly.'

'You know Master Sam—to speak to—
don't you ?' inquired Mr. Oldcastle drily.

He had heard stories of Percy which Sir

Peter had not heard ; not discreditable ones exactly, but certain hints of his 'goings on,' such as a lawyer in a provincial town is pretty sure to hear of a son of his client if at all inclined to fast life.   He knew that he made a point of going to London upon business during the Derby week, and that business required his personal supervision in the north at the time of the Leger.

' Yes, I know him, as you say, to speak to, or rather to nod to,' said Percy indifferently.

' Well, I dare say it's all right—indeed, we have it under Mr. Lyster's hand—but I should just like to have that view confirmed.   If the cheque was paid directly to Mr. Chigwell it could hardly be for value received, and otherwise I don't see how it comes here through his hands.'

' That's true,' said Percy ; ' I'll find it out.'   And he folded the cheque with his usual neatness, and put it in his note-case.

That very evening as he came out of the

pool-room of the local club, he met Mr.
Samuel Chigwell in the street, and considering he only knew him 'to nod to,'
addressed him with considerable familiarity.

'I say, Sam, I want a word with you ;
just walk a few yards with me up Jessops
Lane.'

Having attained this retired spot, Percy
stopped suddenly, laid his hand on the
other's coat collar, and exclaimed in a voice
of suppressed passion :

'What have you been saying about me
to Gerald Lyster, you drunken dog ?'

'Nothing, s'elp me! I never breathed
your name,' replied the other with much
earnestness, but with some difficulty of
articulation.

'But you breathed Jennings's name, which
is worse.'

'Strike me dead if I did ; that is, not as
I know of. I was a little " on " the other
night when we were at billiards at the

Crown together, but not so bad as to do that.'

'You did, I say,' answered the other passionately. 'Gerald knows all about it.'

'It don't follow that I told him,' was the dogged reply. 'There's others as knows it besides me. It's a thing that must come out sooner or later.'

'If it comes out sooner, it will be the worse for you.'

'Now, really, Master Percy, this is very hard,' answered Chigwell, in a tone between a whimper and a whine. 'I give you my word of honour——'

'What ?'

'Well, well—you must let a fellow tell his story his own way. I was no more "on" at the Crown that night than I am at this blessed moment of time.'

He pronounced 'moment' in several syllables, and made his 'blessed' very soft and squashy.

'You drunken beast,' cried Percy

through his teeth, 'what did Lyster give you for telling him ? If you lie, I'll kill you ! And besides, I know the exact sum. It was a cheque for five-and-twenty pounds.'

' That's right. Passable—peaceable—I mean payable, to bearer.'

'So you sold me, did you ? told him all about me and the horses for twenty-five pounds ?'

' Not a word. Not a blooming syllabub —syllable. Might have said Jennings, but don't think so,' said Sam, struggling with a gigantic effort of memory. ' Never mentioned your name, that I'll go to the chop —I mean stake—upon.'

' Then why did he give you the money ?'

' Long account—billiards, drink, bets— all sorts of things. Got tired of waiting. " Pay me what you owe me," says I, " or, by hooky, I'll tell your father." Dying, you know,' added Sam, with a cunning leer, ' which put the screw on, you see, on my young friend.'

' You mean if his father had known what the money was paid for he might have cut him out of his will.'

' Just so ; we are up to snuff, we two.' And he stroked the other's shoulder in a manner that expressed at once conciliation and sympathy.

Percy looked at him with a contempt that seemed uncalled for by so contemptible a creature; the fact was, it was self-contempt. Not because his own behaviour had begotten this familiarity, but because of his folly in having trusted an important secret with such a sot. In his sober moments, however, Mr. Sam Chigwell was a very prudent person, or, as he himself would have expressed it, a ' wide-awake and cautious cuss enough.' Even in his cups he retained a certain sagacity.

' I didn't half like the cheque,' he continued. ' I should have much preferred the shiners ; but as it happened, it was all right. I suppose the old man got soft-hearted at the last. But of course he didn't know that the cheque was coming to me ; and when Gerald heard I had put my name on it he wanted it back again : offered me five stiff uns for it—where he got 'em from nobody knows—but, says I, " Why I ain't a blooming fool, my lad ; I got your cheque changed the same day." '

' A very proper precaution,' said Percy, in modified tones; ' only in future be equally prudent about my affairs as about your own, or you'll get into trouble. I don't threaten twice, mind.'

' I'll be as close as wax, Percy. Your secrets are my own. It's Jennings and Company, and I'm the Co.'

' How are things getting on at the cottage ?' inquired the other abruptly.

' Worse and worse. She is sorry enough, I reckon, that she ever took such pains to catch him. And now there's a young un coming, that makes him more hard upon

26—2

her—as is but natural,' added Mr. Chigwell apologetically.

' Just so,' said Percy drily. ' You are quite sure, by-the-bye, that the marriage was a legal one ?'

' Certain sure. I was there myself. It was the neatest thing. Gerald was sent to town to learn how things were done at your London agent's, and then he combined pleasure with business ; both parties resided in the same parish for the proper time, and had their banns put up all regular. It was his contrivance, not hers, of course ; but she fell into it very easy, and now, poor thing, she wishes it undone. That often comes of marriage, don't it ?'

' I dare say. Now, look you, Chigwell, keep a quiet tongue in your head for the future, and not a word of my having spoken to you to-night, mind that.'

He turned on his heel and walked away without another word.

' Now, that ain't civil,' observed Mr.

Samuel Chigwell, shaking his head re-
proachfully as he watched the other's re-
treating figure. ' Not so much as to say
"Good-evening" to a fellow, far less "Have
a dram?" You're a very clever fellow,
Percy, and you've got better folks than
yourself under your thumb. But there
will be a bust up some day, even with you;
yes, there will, Mister Jennings. And
there's a many as 'ull be glad to see it.'

The next morning, as Gerald was engaged in his room at the mill in his usual
occupation — biting his nails and looking
out of the window at the strong horses
drawing their huge loads up the steep in-
cline of the yard—he saw Percy coming
his way. Under ordinary circumstances
he would have plunged, as it were, head
foremost into the ledger; but since he had
obtained that little loan of his brother-in-
law that was to be, he had grown more
independent. The borrower, in his case,
in place of being the servant of the lender,

had got the upper hand of him, and he did not scruple to show it.

'Well, Percy, how goes it?' inquired the young gentleman, producing a toothpick.

'Do you mean the business? Oh, extending on all sides, like an octopus.'

'The business,' answered Gerald contemptuously. 'What do I care about the business? Though that reminds me,' he added suddenly, 'I am going to care. I think I have been working long enough and hard enough without any share of the profits; and by hook or crook I intend to become a partner.'

'Well, as to that, Gerald,' observed the other, smiling, 'I am only a junior myself, you know. I have no power.'

'You mean that you have not the will,' answered Gerald sulkily. 'I have heard you say that you could do most things for which you had a mind; so just have a mind for this, will you?'

'You shall have my good word, Gerald, when the time comes, you may be sure.'

'That's all very well ; but when will the time come ? I can only say that in the meanwhile I must look to somebody to have it made up to me—that's only fair.'

'Well, well, we'll see what can be done. Your penmanship, I must say' (here he turned over the ledger), ' is first-rate. Your handwriting is ever so much better than your poor father's, and yet sometimes I see a likeness.'

'I never heard that before,' said Gerald surlily.

'It's only occasionally ; but when it's like, it's very like. I don't mean to say it would deceive an expert. Of course you had to practise before you attained perfection ; that is, almost perfection. They are what Mr. Jennings calls trial-gallops.'

'What the deuce do you mean ?'

'Well, it's rather delicate to explain ; but to a person of your keen intelligence, a hint will suffice. Do you recognise this cheque? Not so near, if you please; you have very good eyes, and I don't wish it to be thrown in the fire. It is, or has been, money.'

' I see that.'

'And you have never seen it before ?'

' Never.'

' How curious ! Then I must have been misinformed.'

From white to red, from red to white again, and then to a leaden grey, with moisture on it, grew Gerald's face. But his voice was confident as brass, as he once more repeated, ' Never.'

' The story I have heard,' continued Percy, his eyes on him with relentless scorn, 'is that you gave this cheque to Sam Chigwell in discharge for a debt you owed him.'

' Sam is a liar, as everybody knows. The cheque is to bearer : who knows to whom my father gave it?'

' In your very natural excitement and apprehensions,' observed Percy coldly, 'you have lost sight of your business habits. The cheque is crossed ; here is Sam's name at the back of it.'

' And what if it is ?'

' It shows it came into his hands, and, as he is prepared to swear, from you.'

' And what if it did ?'

'Well, it shows that other people are liars besides Sam, for you have just said you had never seen it. However, that's nothing. Sam is prepared to swear that you wanted to buy it back again with five five-pound notes—*my* notes most probably. I don't blame you, for that would have been worth the money to you, my friend, ten times told. I don't wonder you were so anxious to assist your father of late in his private affairs. I don't wonder that you were so anxious and excited in your manner that some people really began to give you credit for filial sorrow.'

· 'I deny everything,' said Gerald doggedly.

'Very good; that is, you reserve your
defence. In that case the Bank has no
alternative but to prosecute you for forgery.'

Gerald staggered and sat down; or
rather he fell backwards into a chair,
where he lay huddled up like a heap of
clothes, but with his frightened eyes fixed
mechanically upon his persecutor. His lips
essayed to speak, but could only murmur
the name of Mr. Oldcastle.

'Quite right,' said Percy approvingly.
'As being a friend of the family, Mr. Oldcastle would naturally wish to avoid exposure; but then he is a lawyer also, and
would never compound a felony. No,
there is only one way out of it that I can
see,' he added thoughtfully.

'A way out of it—what way?' exclaimed
the wretched youth. 'I'd pay the money
twenty times over to have it squared.'

'Squared. One would think the matter

in hand was forty shillings or six weeks,
instead of penal servitude. Your only
chance, sir, is to plead guilty.'

' But then I shall be sent to prison.'

' Not necessarily ; no, I think I can stop
that. When I said "plead guilty," I only
meant make a clean breast of it. I have
brought a little slip of writing, in case I
found you in a sensible frame of mind.
It is a full acknowledgment of your error,
that's all. But you'll have to sign it.'

'And then you'll destroy the cheque !'
exclaimed Gerald eagerly.

' I shall tell Mr. Oldcastle that I have
destroyed it, which will be the same thing.
He does not know what I know; he
has only his suspicions. I shall tell him
that I have made inquiries and found
them groundless.'

' And the Bank ?'

' What can the Bank do without the
cheque ?'

' I'll sign it,' gasped Gerald. ' And

henceforth I'll never bother you—I won't, upon my word, Percy—about Jennings.'

' I'm quite sure you won't,' said Percy grimly, as Gerald signed it.

CHAPTER XXIII.

MR. LYSTER'S affairs were left in a condition so intricate, as Mr. Oldcastle expressed it, that their settlement seemed indefinitely postponed. To all Sir Peter's inquiries, which were numerous, the lawyer had one answer: 'I do not know, myself.' He protested that his late client had dabbled in pretty nearly everything, and that what he might be worth was for the present incalculable. This last word was a very satisfactory one to Sir Peter, who characteristically associated it with untold wealth instead of affixing to it its legitimate meaning. When closely pressed as to the possible sum, the lawyer resolutely shook his head.

'You must surely know within a few thousand pounds,' persisted Sir Peter.

'No, sir,' said Mr. Oldcastle, 'nor yet within twenty thousand ;' which was strictly true, since even that amount might turn out to be a drop in the ocean of his late client's liabilities as respected his unlimited ventures. Sir Peter never suspected that the sum might be a minus quantity, and in Mr. Oldcastle's opinion it was not his business to enlighten him. He entertained a great regard for Clare, whose happiness, he perceived, was in Percy's keeping, and his object was to do his best for the young couple. He had a lawyer's regard for agreements ; and that notion which he perceived Sir Peter had in his head of the marriage being made dependent upon how Clare was 'left,' offended his sense of right. Mr. Oldcastle would not perhaps have been so solicitous that the course of true love

should run smooth, had he entertained the
same opinion of Mr. Percy Fibbert as of
yore. But since Mr. Lyster's death he
had seen a good deal of the young man,
and was inclined to dismiss certain prejudices he had formed against him. Though
a man of the world, he was no student of
human nature, and did not understand how
light a thing self-interest is when weighed
against the promptings of passion; it
seemed to him a fine thing in Percy that
he should have 'stuck to his guns,' by
which he meant to Clare, in spite of the
pecuniary dangers that encompassed her.
He was accustomed to look at matters
objectively, just as they really stood, and
did not comprehend how so excellent a
business man as Percy took, as a lover, so
sanguine and rose-coloured a view of them.
He also lost sight of the fact, or, we should
rather say, of the value set on it by the
ambitious Percy, that the bulk of Clare's
money being invested in the firm would

give her husband, for the time at least, a far more powerful voice in it than he had yet possessed. On the whole, in short, he took him to be a disinterested lover.

Moreover, he was very favourably impressed with his conduct towards Gerald. He had asked him 'How about the cheque?' and Percy had given him an evasive answer.

'But I must know, my dear sir, if there is anything wrong about it. It is a mere question of duty. If Sam Chigwell has obtained that cheque improperly, his being poor Lyster's cousin shall not screen him from the consequences.'

'Sam Chigwell was not to blame in the matter,' replied Percy, with a pained look.

'That is as good as saying that some one else was.'

'It was a disreputable transaction upon somebody's part,' admitted Percy unwillingly, 'but it would be better—much better—to say nothing about it.'

'My dear young sir, I appreciate your motives, but this is a business affair. As Mr. Lyster's executor I must at least know whether that cheque was honestly come by.'

'I am sorry to say,' answered Percy, quietly, 'that I must decline to answer that question. The cheque is burnt.'

'Burnt! Who burnt it?'

'I did. It is, as you say, a business affair; and here is the twenty-five pounds, which makes all square.'

'And you are paying that sum out of your own pocket?'

'Well,' said Percy, with a forced smile, 'it is your duty to take it as a part of the estate, but not to ask embarrassing questions. However, between ourselves, I am. Pray, let us say no more about it.'

Mr. Oldcastle shook his head as he took the notes, but he did take them. That Gerald had behaved in some disreputable way, he was well convinced, and he was far from wishing to know the details. On the other hand, Percy seemed to have behaved admirably; and that young gentleman, who had the cheque quite safe in his notebook, was very well satisfied with what had taken place. ' I have scratched a horse before now,' he said to himself, ' but never paid forfeit to such advantage.' He felt that Gerald was more under his thumb than ever, while he had secured a powerful advocate upon his side in many ways, but especially with Clare.

If that young lady, indeed, had been of the other sex, it would have been difficult for her to resist the arguments which were addressed to her in favour of an early marriage. Mr. Oldcastle was in favour of it on material grounds. He wished to see his client's daughter safely mated with the near relative of one so powerful as Sir Peter; the palladium of whose money and influence would protect her—even if the worst came to the worst (which, however,

he was far from anticipating), with respect
to those investments. Percy, by this time,
felt justified in pressing the point with the
ardour of a lover. And even Gerald,
though it could hardly be said with much
force of natural eloquence, expressed to
her his opinion that it was ' deuced hard on
a young fellow to be kept on and off,' as
Percy was.

A decent interval had now elapsed since
her loss, and it seemed reasonable enough
that she should turn her thoughts towards
matrimony, instead of casting backward
glances, as it were, upon the tomb. But,
being a woman, argument and reason, even
though her own feelings seconded their
efforts, were powerless against sentiment.
The voice of her father's disapprobation
still rang in her ears, though, doubtless
with failing strength, she still pleaded for
time. Perhaps, too, Mr. Percy Fibbert, in
this matter, had been hoist by his own
petard; his having told her of Mildred's

passion for him, having put Clare on her mettle. It is just possible that she said to herself :

'Since he loves me he can wait for me ; nor am I afraid that any woman shall rob me of him in the meantime.'

To Miss Darrell, to whom she had often spoken upon the subject generally, one may be sure she said nothing of this. She only affirmed that her heart was for the present too sore with sorrow to permit her to think of love. It was rather unsatisfactory that to these protestations the little old lady confined herself in her replies to ' Just so,' and ' Indeed.' Talkative enough upon other matters, she was very reticent upon this one, nor did she even volunteer one syllable of advice. To Herbert Newton, however, she was less reserved. His scientific invention had not yet been brought to perfection, the weather being still very unfavourable to subaqueous experiments, and he had therefore postponed his departure for South America, and was still an occasional visitor at the Lodge.

One afternoon, when Miss Darrell and the young engineer happened to be alone together, 'Does Clare ever talk to you about her marriage?' inquired the old lady bluntly.

'To *me !* Good heavens ! I mean,' he added, repenting of the astonishment in his tone, which he saw had excited hardly less surprise in his companion, 'it would be surely strange if she did so. Young women don't usually talk to young men about such things.'

'But you are her cousin, and her father's dearest friend,' replied the other, shutting one of her bright eyes, and threading her needle with deft deliberation, 'why shouldn't she ?'

'For that very reason,' answered Herbert quietly: 'her father never took to Percy; and she naturally imagines that I may share his prejudices.'

' And do you ?'

' Well, speaking for oneself one does not call one's dislikes prejudices ; but I do not like Percy Fibbert.'

' That is frank, at all events. Your ways are always above board, that I will say for you. I don't believe,' said the old lady, smiling, 'that you will ever be able to breathe under water, Herbert. You must let some one else make your experiments for you. However, I think I know why you don't like our young friend.'

' Indeed,' said Herbert, with an answering smile, and in a tone of affected indifference, ' that is very clever of you.'

' Yes ; the reason is——' and she paused here, which was cruel of the old lady, since the poor lad was blushing scarlet, 'that you and Percy are so different in this matter ; I mean as to plain sailing, he tacks a good deal ; *I* call him Percy Fibber.'

' I am not going to say a word against him,' said Herbert, resolutely.

'Of course not, *noblesse oblige;* but you know that he tells stories. He told one yesterday to Clare.'

'It is just possible,' said Herbert.

'Well, there now, I should never have thought you could have been so bitter. But this was not an ordinary story, it was a bolder flight of the imagination than usual; and what's more I don't think Clare believes it.'

'Indeed.' His tone so far from being indifferent had this time a good deal of interest in it.

'Yes; it is the first occasion, perhaps, that Clare had had suspicions of his veracity; but they are certainly aroused. He was pressing his suit, as usual, importuning her (as I must say he has some right to do) to name the day for their marriage; and she, also as usual, was pleading the newness of her sorrow, which is really not now so very new. "What you mean," he said, getting, I fancy, a little out of temper, "is

that you can't forget your father's objections to our union. That they existed at
one time I do not deny, but I · do assure
you, Clare, he surmounted them. He told
me so with his own lips." '

'That is a lie,' cried Herbert, vehemently.

'Hush, hush! Some people think that
all things are fair in love and war; let us
call it a stratagem. Of course Mr. Fibber
was very particular as to the date of the
interview in which Mr. Lyster withdrew
his opposition. It was December the 7th.
Clare told me that Percy and her father
had a long talk together on that day.'

'That was true,' assented Herbert.

'I supposed so. Percy is not a man to
go wrong as to circumstance. But as to
the main fact, Clare is doubtful; Percy's
assertion has had a very painful effect on
her. I told her that she should endeavour
to place herself in the young man's position,
and not be too hard upon him.'

'Then I think you did very wrong,' put
in Herbert, bluntly.

Miss Darrell looked at him with twink-
ling eyes. 'How odd it is that scientific
folks are always so simple,' she said. 'The
mathematical master in my school, to whom
algebra was easy, and was understood to
know something even of logarithms, could
never understand when the girls were
laughing at him. Not that I am laughing at you, Mr. Herbert, of course. But
is it possible that you, to whom creating
a vacuum is, I suppose, quite a common
occurrence, can imagine that Mr. Percy
Fibber is likely to profit by any advocacy
of mine; or that defending him to Clare is
the way to further his interest with her.'

'I should certainly say that it was the
way.'

'Goo—d heavens,' exclaimed the old
lady, 'and this is the man who is going to
teach us to breathe under water! Why
a child of fourteen—that is a girl child—

would know that to take a woman's part in
a quarrel with her lover is to turn her
complaint into approval, and to reunite
them at once.'

' I did not know you wished them to be
disunited.'

' Nor would you ever have guessed it
had I not told you. I flatter myself Clare
does not know it herself; but I do wish it
nevertheless.'

' It is no use wishing, however,' sighed
Herbert.

' No. But thanks to what Mr. Fibber,
when speaking of it to me has termed
" Clare's exquisite sensitiveness," and, when
speaking of it to himself—for I happened
to hear him once on the landing—her
" infernal obstinacy," we have still time
upon our side ; and the longer she knows
Percy as a lover the better chance she has
of finding him out, and rejecting him, as a
husband.'

' She will never do that now,' sighed

Herbert, 'since she clove to him when her father was alive, and spoke to her against the match.'

'My dear Mr. Herbert, you may under- stand steam locomotion, but it is quite plain you know nothing of the workings of a woman's mind. There is an old riddle that compares our sex to ivy because "the greater the ruin the closer it clings" (one of your cynical sex has answered it the other way, "the closer it clings the greater the ruin;" that's rubbish). I don't say the more worthless a man is the more a good girl loves him, but the more he is abused the more, unquestionably, she feels inclined to stand by him. In my opinion—and I ought to know something of girls' minds—Percy has not advanced in Clare's good graces since your uncle's death.'

'But, my dear madam, they are engaged to be married.'

'And you've been engaged as deputy assistant acting engineer to the Pernambuco

railway any time within the last six months,
yet here you are still at Stokeville ?'

' But that's because my experiments are
not finished.'

' And perhaps some one else is trying
experiments.'

' What ! do you really think Clare has
doubts of him ?   Oh, my dear Miss Darrell,
if you knew what I think—I do not say of
Percy ; I do not wish to speak of any man
behind his back—but the apprehensions I
entertain for Clare's happiness, which I believe is about to be entrusted to unsafe
hands ! I ventured once, with no sinister
or selfish intention, Heaven knows, to say
as much.   I told her she was throwing herself away.   I warned her that a day would
come when she would think as much.'

' You did, did you ?' cried the old lady,
throwing up her hands. ' And this is a
man who makes railways. One of those
to whose intelligence and foresight honest
folks entrust themselves whenever they go

a journey. It's enough to make the poorest take post-horses. Clare may marry, sir— partly thanks to you—of course she will find out her mistake ; but if she confesses it, after what you have said to her, and to *you*, I'll swallow this case of needles. Pray go away—go to the—the Junction. Black yourself, oil yourself, attend to your business, but don't come here (unless you can keep your mouth shut) till I send for you. It may be Clare will want your help.'

' Clare ! Oh, Miss Darrell, if I could but serve her.'

' Of course. I know all that. I said, it *may* be. If we want you, I'll send for you —the idea of your having told her *that ;* no wonder she keeps you at arm's length. *I* would if I were she ; go away, sir. You'll do no harm ? You'll never speak ? I am not so sure of that ; indeed you've spoken enough, and done harm enough, to last a professional mischief-maker for his natural life. Go away, sir.'

CHAPTER XXIV.

ON THE BRINK.

EVEN the richest men have their weaknesses, and that of Sir Peter Fibbert was 'temper.' Unlike a fire he was easily put out, but by no means so easily put in again, and the difference between fair weather and foul was very marked with him. When he didn't joke he stormed. The least thing would do it; a kink in the machinery of the mill; a scowl from 'a hand' dismissed—a very different thing from that 'vanished hand,' the touch of which the poet missed so ;—a fall in the cotton market; the omission of his man to brush his hat, or a disagreeable business letter. It was this last misfortune that put him in ill-humour one morning when at breakfast, as usual, with his daughter and Percy. He had received news of the commercial failure of a village linendraper, which meant a bad debt to the firm of perhaps twenty pounds, and the state of Sir Peter's money market was always what is technically termed 'sensitive.'

'What the deuce people mean by failing in this outrageous way I can't think,' exclaimed the outraged knight. 'Here's a fellow starts with nothing; asks us for credit; speculates with our goods, loses them, and then comes out of the bankruptcy court as white as snow.'

'It reminds me of our own manufacturing process,' smiled Percy, 'except that "the devil" has him at last instead of at first.'

'I see nothing to laugh at, sir,' cried Sir Peter, incensed at this ill-timed jest on the loss of good money. 'What it reminds

you of I don't know, but it reminds me
that the affairs of the firm want looking to.
It is most abominable that in the only
good time we have had for years, or are
likely to have, a third of our profits should
go to a dead man, who can do no stroke of
work to help us. For my part I think it
something worse than discreditable, since
he only lived a few minutes into the
current year, that such a quibble should
be taken advantage of by his family.'

'Well, really, sir, if Mr. Lyster had
lived a few minutes *short* of the necessary
time,' urged Percy ; 'you wouldn't have
called it a quibble to take advantage——'

'Hold your tongue, sir,' exclaimed Sir
Peter, vehemently. 'I should have done
everything that was right and proper in that
case, as in any other. I use the word discreditable, in connection with Mr. Lyster's
affairs, advisedly. If everything was correct
and above-board, should we have Mr.
Oldcastle shaking his head and declining

to talk about them, even in confidence, to his own client? It's my belief that the man has left next to nothing, except the money in the business.'

'I am quite certain, Sir Peter, that is not the case,' said Percy firmly.

'Then what *is* the case? For if you think that Clare's thirty thousand pounds— no, begad, it's twenty, for Newton holds ten of it—will satisfy my just expectations, I mean as regards you, you're deucedly mistaken. Our agreement was that the girl was to be *bona fide* well provided for.'

'But her share of the profits, sir, during the present year——'

'How dare you talk to me of her share in the profits?' broke in Sir Peter. 'How dare you remind me that she is picking my pocket? Yes, sir, you are going to get your wife's dowry out of your uncle's purse.'

At the word 'wife,' Mildred, sitting

quietly behind the tea-urn as her custom was in these domestic commotions, set her lips together and flashed a fiery glance at Percy.

'No doubt, sir,' admitted that young gentleman, 'Mr. Lyster's death was most inopportune for all parties except his own family. But it is hard that I should be held accountable for it.'

'Yes, it's very hard, no doubt,' sneered Sir Peter, rising, 'that you should be com-pelled to accept—if all things go as they should do,' he added, parenthetically, and as it almost seemed in spite of himself, 'something like a hundred thousand pounds. But I daresay you'll contrive to bear it. What is it to you if Swaffham here has failed for I don't know how much?'

Percy might reasonably have replied that it was as hard proportionally for him as for Sir Peter, or even have suggested that Swaffham was not a man whose misfortunes would seriously affect the firm of Fibbert and Lyster; but he was too glad to get rid of his uncle on any terms to detain him by argument. He only wished he could have got rid of his cousin also.

'What is this?' said Mildred in cold incisive tones, when her father had left them, 'about Clare's having a hundred thousand pounds?'

'It is mere moonshine, my dear; Sir Peter is too much in the habit of counting his chickens before they're hatched. Mr. Lyster's share in the business may no doubt produce a considerable profit; perhaps one-tenth of what Sir Peter chooses to put it at; but it may also produce nothing, or less than nothing. The fact is, your father is much too sanguine; in my opinion the revival in trade already shows signs of slackening, and our liabilities are something enormous.'

'I don't want to hear about trade,' said Mildred, fixing her eyes suspiciously on her cousin, 'I want to hear about Clare.'

'There is nothing to tell more than I have already told you, my dear Mildred. At present she still holds me to my word, and while she does that, you know as well as I do, that I am powerless. At the same time I am doing my best to put off the evil day. Do you suppose that it is her fault that no day has yet been named for our marriage ?'

'No, indeed, I don't suppose that,' said Mildred, bitterly.

'Well, it's some comfort to feel that you at least give me credit for good intentions. If I dared to do more than procrastinate, I should precipitate a catastrophe. Coldness and delay may effect our object, but should it once be guessed, it is as likely as not that Clare would come straight to your father and denounce us both. I shrink from picturing to myself what might happen to us then ; the very best would be

that Sir Peter would insist on my marrying
the girl within the week so as to render our
hopes impossible.'

' And you call that " the very best," do
you ?' exclaimed Mildred.

' My dear child,' said Percy gravely, ' I
have always been frank with you—duplicity
is not in my nature—and I confess that I
would rather lose you than drag you down
with me to irretrievable ruin. That is
what a quarrel between me and your father
means, and—for your own dear sake—I
will never risk it.'

Mildred bit her lips and frowned, but
Percy felt that for the time he had con-
quered. His victory, however, had been
obtained, as it were, with a dead lift, and
the next conflict might have a less favour-
able result. Such struggles, indeed, were
almost too much even for his iron nerve
and front of brass, and had become to be
intolerable.

' What did you say to her last ?' inquired Mildred, with downcast eyes, her taper fingers tracing out the pattern on the table-cloth.

'To Clare? Well, I spoke of her father; the old man never liked me, you know, and I find that subject is my best protector. I talked to her of the last interview he and I had together, and affected to deplore his obstinacy. She is never very sweet upon me after a reminder of that sort.'

' Hypocrite !'

The observation was uttered with such extreme sharpness and energy, that for the moment Percy was taken aback. He really thought that the injurious epithet had for some inexplicable reason been applied to himself instead of Clare, for whom it was, of course, intended.

' And there are some people,' continued Mildred, ' who call that girl simple. In my opinion there is no such thing as a simple girl.'

'They're rare, no doubt,' assented Percy; 'and simple women still rarer. There's one of that sort now at Oak Lodge. One of those "honest, old-fashioned creatures," who are in reality deeper than all the rest. A Miss Darrell.'

'She was a governess, or something of that sort, was she not?' said Mildred, indifferently.

'Yes; she has taken up her old trade again, if I am not mistaken, and aspires to govern Clare. A very dangerous little old woman, in my opinion.'

'Of course, she endeavours to egg Clare on to entrap you.'

'Just so; she never leaves a stone unturned to effect that object. Her notion is to procure a comfortable home for herself, and to rule the roast when—I mean, in case her efforts should prove successful. What a very pretty ring you have got on, my darling; that's something new, is it not?'

'Yes; but I don't admire it. Mr. Farrer gave it me.'

'Oh dear me. On your engaged finger, too! Now, if you were in my place, here would be a fine opportunity for a scene. Confess, if Clare had given me a ring, what a row there would have been about it.'

'I'll throw it in the fire,' cried Mildred, pulling at the ring.

'No, you won't, darling, at least not to please me,' said Percy, softly, and taking her hand in his. 'It looks very pretty where it is, and I do assure you I don't mind; I understand the necessity of circumstances, and bow to it. I am not jealous.'

'No, because you are so conceited,' said Mildred, with pretended indignation, but secretly melted by his caressing tone. The touch of his hand had all the influence of the mesmerist. 'You cannot picture to yourself that you have really a rival?'

'No, I can't, Mildred—at least with *you*,' he added, dropping his voice to a

whisper. ' Whatever happens, I am afraid
I shall never be persuaded of that.'

She knew very well what he meant;
that even if she married Frank Farrer she
would still hold her cousin dearer than her
husband. Yet she made no attempt to
reprove him, not because she admitted the
fact (though she did do so), but because
her literature had undermined her prin-
ciples; she felt that it was 'naughty' in
Percy, but when young ladies begin to call
things 'naughty' they soon forget that they
are wrong. On the whole, indeed, such
was the perversion of her mind, that the
young man's imprudent speech flattered
her vanity instead of being a proof of his.
As to Percy, he felt that it was a great
point gained that she had received that
' whatever happens' without an explosion.
It led him to hope that when his marriage
actually took place, Mildred would bring
herself to endure it without creating a
public scandal. But her manner on this

occasion, not to mention that of Sir Peter,
urged him to bring matters to a head at all
hazards. The account he had given Mildred of his last interview with Clare was,
as we are aware, anything but a correct
one ; indeed, it was the very reverse of
correct. It was true, however, he had
spoken of her father, with the result with
which Miss Darrell has made us acquainted. He knew that his attempt to
persuade Clare that Mr. Lyster had been
reconciled to their engagement had failed
for the present ; but he had other means
of convincing her which could scarcely fail.
The use of them, it was true, was a little
dangerous, but disappointment and delay
had made him desperate. If it had not
been so, certain news which was communicated to him that morning would
certainly have given him pause. As he
passed by Mr. Oldcastle's window, on his
way through the town, the lawyer beckoned
him in.

'You will be glad to hear I have got the Delver Mine Company wound up. Of course there has been a loss, but nothing to speak of, and we have got rid of all responsibility.'

'That is good indeed,' cried Percy. 'Yet Sir Peter told me you shook your head yesterday when he asked how affairs were getting on, and that has excited his suspicions.'

'I can't help that, young gentleman,' answered the lawyer gravely. ' I can hold my tongue when duty, all things considered, seems to demand my silence ; but to smirk and smile when your uncle—one of my own clients, too—asks questions about Mr. Lyster's investments, is not to be expected. It would be an act of hypocrisy, of which he would have good reason to complain— a clear case of *suggestio falsi.* There is still that bank, you know.'

' It's a very little one.'

' Yes ; and it has done very little business. Its liabilities, it is true, I have reason to believe are proportionally small, but, such as they are, Mr. Lyster's estate is responsible for them. The other proprietors are mere men of straw.'

'What a risky old fool he must have been ?'

'No, it wasn't that; he was not a fool, far from it. But when one has lost money, even the wisest of us are sometimes seized with a sort of desperation to get it back again at all risks.'

'To plunge ? I know it,' said Percy naïvely.

'Well, what you probably do not know, the desire is far stronger when you have lost money belonging to other people.'

'You don't mean to say Lyster did that.'

'Not in a fraudulent sense; an honester man never drew breath. But he did not consider his money to be his own so much as Clare's ; and what he had saved for her he had lost. If he had not had the great good luck to live into the present year, and share in the profits of your firm, he might have left his daughter almost destitute.'

'But she has twenty thousand in the firm.'

'In the eyes of the law she has thirty thousand.'

'How's that? I thought ten thousand was Newton's.'

'So it is, of course; but there is no legal document to prove it. It is quite astounding how so clever a man as Herbert Newton should have permitted things to be done so loosely. When he came of age he seems to have handed his money over to his uncle to place in the business without so much as an acknowledgment.'

'What a born idiot!'

'Well, it was at all events imprudent; you would certainly not have behaved so to *your* uncle.'

Percy threw up his head and his hands
as though he would have said : ' Am I a
madman ?'

' So if this unlimited bank should fail,'
continued Mr. Oldcastle, ' poor Newton's
money is actually liable to be swept away
as though it were a portion of his uncle's
estate.'

' Of course he knows nothing of this
himself ?' observed Percy.

' Newton ?   He knows everything.   It
was my bounden duty to tell him.   He
took it as cool as a cucumber ; one would
really have supposed he had been prepared
for it.   That he could hardly have been,
however ; his uncle had left him a letter
which he was to have had if Mr. Lyster
had not lived to the first of January, and
the contents of which I can now guess at,
as Newton assuredly can ; but it was of
course never delivered.   Though Clare, of
course, would never let him be wronged of
a penny if she could help it, Newton has

positively declined for the present to have matters set right. He will see how they turn out, he says. As it happens, there is no real danger to his interests. I have taken measures to prevent any further mischief; the bank will presently be wound up like the mine; and our total liability, if things come to the very worst, will not exceed fifteen thousand pounds. What might have happened had I not interfered when I did Heaven only knows; poor Lyster certainly never knew; he was for the last months of his life, I am now persuaded, consumed with terrible apprehensions.'

'Serve him right,' said Percy, contemptuously.

'Well, yes; it did serve him right, but he suffered enough for his folly. You now understand that expression you found upon his dying face, and why his eyes were fixed upon the clock hands. He felt that his daughter had escaped from penury, and that his nephew's money was safe. During those last five minutes he was comparatively a happy man.'

' That is very satisfactory,' said Percy, drily. ' But even as matters stand, it is possible, then, that poor Clare may have nothing left but her share in the business, minus fifteen thousand pounds—that is a surplus of fifteen thousand.'

' Only five thousand ; ten belongs to Newton.'

' To be sure ; only five thousand.'

' However,' continued the lawyer, ' matters can hardly turn out so badly as that. Moreover, she has five-sixths of her father's estate, but that will be but a modicum when we subtract what has been dropped in the mine.'

' I see,' said Percy, thoughtfully ; his mind was full of anger against the dead man, and of disappointment on his own account. But his heart—or those desires which occupy that region in so many of us

—was still fixed on marrying Clare. If
Newton was foolish enough to leave his
money unsecured the law would give it to
Clare's husband ; and when once his wife
he would find arguments to persuade her
to keep it. And even if it slipped through
his fingers, what was ten thousand pounds
compared with her share of that bounteous
year in the profits of Fibbert and Lyster ?
She would still be a great heiress, though
her fortune would fall far short of Sir
Peter's expectations. If, however, his
uncle should get to know about that bank,
he would certainly put that spoke in his
wheel which he had often threatened to do,
and forbid the marriage ; and once set free
of his engagement, what trouble he would
have with Mildred !

Upon the whole he decided to play his
trump card — one that involved all the
danger of exposing a revoke, but which if
it passed unchallenged would win the game
for him—that very day.

CHAPTER XXV.

THERE are some folks who have a horror of lying and nothing else; who are themselves so honest that they take a genuine pleasure in telling the truth however unpleasant it may be to their fellow-creatures; who make no allowance for dependence, poverty, or any other miserable circumstance which suggests 'the weapon of weakness,' and by whom every unhappy wight whom they have once caught in a falsehood is from henceforth anathematised. Such persons are sometimes worse, as they are often more disagreeable, than the offenders on whom they pass such sentence. But, notwithstanding this, Truth is, on the whole, the touchstone of character. Wherever there is a want of it, there is something else wanting in the moral sense ; and where it abides there is strength.

Clare Lyster had passed too much of her life in active benevolence, to be hard on those who (though, poor souls, with little art) attempt ' to make the thing that is not as the thing that is.' She could make allowance for human necessity (or what seems to be so), and separate the offender from his crime. But when there was no necessity, nor evil custom bred of patronage, she was in all offences against truth a perfect Draco.

It was not woman's jealousy so much as her innate horror of duplicity, that set her so against Mildred, to whom, after Percy's revelations of her schemes, she could hardly trust herself to speak, for, to herself, even concealment, much more deception, was difficult. What Percy had told her about that young lady she believed implicitly. It was her nature to trust until she had found reason to distrust; and she could even hope against hope, as she had done in Gerald's case, to find truth even in the most unpromising moral strata. Kinship and duty had fought long and hard for him with her : and even now, though trust was gone, she pitied him as much as she blamed him. But with Percy it was different ; her love had invested him with an atmosphere of its own, through which she saw him not as he was at all ; and nothing but his own act could have dispelled it.

Percy's sagacity had, as we know, led him to suspect that on the day of Mr. Lyster's death he had made some last appeal to Clare to induce her to break with him. He even believed that it was the remembrance of that final interview, more than any general sense of her father's disfavour to him, which now caused her to

withhold her consent to name a day for
their marriage. And yet, in the teeth of
this he had ventured to assert that Mr.
Lyster, on a certain date, had, in a private
conversation with himself, formally withdrawn his objections.

This Clare did not believe. On the
other hand she was very far from imputing
to Percy a direct falsehood. She thought
it probable that her father had, to her lover,
used much gentler terms in speaking of the
matter than he had done to others, or even
to herself, while Percy, on his part, had
retailed to her what he said with a certain
natural but unconscious colouring.

'I am well aware, dear Percy,' she said,
'that my father gave consent to our
marriage ; but he did so unwillingly and
because he saw that his daughter's happiness demanded it—as it does still. Oh,
Percy, give me time. You do not know
what a struggle it is for me. How love
and duty rend my poor heart.'

'There is no reason for their doing so,
my darling,' he had answered. 'They
should be both on one side. I do not
pretend to say that I was a favourite with
your poor father, but he confessed to me
with his own lips that he had allowed his
prejudices to influence him too strongly;
and that in our marriage I should have his
best wishes and you his blessing.'

'Then why did you never tell me so
before?'

The tone was such as Clare had never
used to him before, nor dreamt of using;
as unmistakably incredulous, as though
she had said, 'if this had been so you
would have certainly told me of it
before.'

Percy had answered very softly, 'I had
hoped that such an argument would have
been unnecessary; I trusted to our mutual
love to find its own way with you; it is
only because I find you inexorable that I
bring myself to advance this plea. It is a

humiliation. But I would do anything to win you.'

She looked at him with yearning eyes, but which yet had some suspicion in them. Since he confessed that he would 'do anything' to attain his end, perhaps he would even tell a falsehood.

'You do not believe me, even now,' he continued, bitterly. 'I suppose I must bring you the proof.'

'What proof?'

'Only of your lover's truth and honesty, which it seems you doubt. I am humiliated already, why should I not be abased?'

Clare did not reply to this, which he was far from being displeased at; nor at that time did he repeat his offer.

'It seems so strange,' she said, not so much apologetically as thoughtfully; 'I cannot understand it;' and Percy felt, not only that his weapon had missed its aim, but had recoiled upon himself.

At the time, as we have said, he made

no further attempt to shake Clare's con-
victions, but when he came to reflect he
recognised the danger of leaving things as
they were. If his statement was not reiterated she would naturally construe his
silence unfavourably—she would hold him
to have tried to impose upon her, and to
have given up the attempt as a failure.
On the other hand, to reiterate the statement and be again discredited might be
fatal.

In the meantime came Percy's interview
with his uncle and Mildred, and his talk
with Mr. Oldcastle, both combining to
convince him that there was no time to
be lost in his wooing, or rather his winning.
It was a desperate case and required a
desperate remedy.

He walked to Oak Lodge that
morning, instead of, as usual, taking a
vehicle or riding, in order to consider the
matter at leisure, and from no point of
view had it an agreeable aspect. The

element of risk, however, which would have dismayed most men, however audacious, weighed with him but lightly, even if it had not a certain attraction. The idea of giving Clare up, or, as I am sorry to say it presented itself to him, 'of letting her go to the devil,' only occurred to him to be summarily dismissed. 'And if she gives *me* up,' he grimly soliloquized, 'it will not be my fault ;' concerning which observation, however, perhaps one may venture to say that there were two opinions.

He found Clare looking graver and sadder than usual, of which his sagacity failed to explain the reason ; he flattered himself, especially as she also looked kind and pitiful, that she repented of her incredulity ; whereas she was sorrowing for his own fault, for which she had nevertheless forgiven him.

'I hope, my darling,' said he, as he pressed her to his breast, 'that you have been thinking differently of me in my absence than you thought or seemed to think of me when we spoke together yesterday.'

'Do not let us talk of that, I beg of you,' sighed Clare.

'I do not wish to do so,' he answered gently. 'I only want the assurance that you do not longer deem me capable of a deception.'

'None of us are incapable of deceiving ourselves, Percy,' was the grave reply.

'If you mean that my version of your father's words was an incorrect one,' he said, 'or even coloured by my own wishes, I must be allowed to deny it. I cannot submit to such an imputation.'

She sighed again, and gazed through the window on the gravel path on which her father used to be wheeled in his chair to enjoy the wintry sunshine. Her face and her silence convinced him that he had lost ground with her, and it had become so necessary to gain ground! The moment had arrived for his *coup d'état.*

' I am not accustomed, my dear Clare,' he said, with gentle gravity, ' to find my word called in question by anybody, and from you least of all did I anticipate such a thing. When I said that such and such was the case—even if it was an unlikely thing—I had hoped that that would have been sufficient for you. Even now I cannot but think it would have been so but for evil counsel and detraction. Nay, hear me out,' for she had moved her head, in the negative, and seemed about to speak. ' Whether this be so or not, it seems your lover's word of honour requires some corroboration. I had hoped that would have been unnecessary, but it shall have it. Your poor father, it seems, knew you better than I did. On the day after my interview with him he wrote me a letter, with the object, as I now believe, of its being shown to you in case of necessity (such as has now arisen), reiterating what he had expressed to me with his own lips.

Is it still necessary that you should see it ?'

' A letter !' she said, eagerly, and taking no notice of this last inquiry. ' A letter in his own hand !'

' Certainly. What use,' he added bitterly, ' would a message from him have been ? You would only have said that I invented it, or suborned the messenger.'

' Percy ! Percy !'

' I am sorry to wound you, Clare ; but you must remember how you have wounded *me*. Here is the letter ; you recognise the handwriting, I suppose. You do not suspect me of forgery ?'

She took the letter, sobbing bitterly ; and kissed it. It must have been the last letter, she reflected, her father had ever written ; the words were formed a little irregularly, as with a weak and failing hand, but were quite legible, and in his well-known hand.

' DEAR PERCY,

' I have nothing more to say than I
said to you yesterday morning. But something prompts me to reiterate it. It may
be a satisfaction to you—and to another—
to have my approval of your marriage, for
my consent has already been given under
my own hand. I have had, it is true,
certain prejudices to surmount; but now
they no longer exist—that is, they do not
do so to-day. As I grow weaker (for I am
a dying man), they may recur. I take this
opportunity, therefore, while it is yet afforded me, to accept you unreservedly as a
son-in-law. I bequeath my darling daughter to your tender keeping; I charge you
to love and honour her; and in all matters
of advice and guardianship to fill my place.
Whatever ill I may have imputed to you, I
have never accused you of covetousness.
I believe you love my darling for her own
sake. Whether my failing strength will
carry me into the next year or not—upon

which hang such important consequences
to her as regards fortune—will, I feel,
make no difference in your intentions
towards her. She will be yours in any
case. That she will have my blessing she
is well convinced, and be assured that it
will also attend your union with her. I
enjoin you to look after Gerald. When
Herbert goes abroad there will be no one
but yourself to exercise any influence over
him, and he will need a firm hand. As to
Clare, should my partnership continue, I
know her interests will be well attended to.
I never impugned your business capacities,
Percy; and I now hereby withdraw my
objections to you in all other respects.

'Yours faithfully, .

'JOHN LYSTER.'

Clare read the letter over to herself with
great attention; her tears had ceased,
though one or two had fallen when she
came upon the tender references to herself.

Then she rose up and kissed her lover.

'I have done you wrong, Percy.'

'Nay, dear Clare, say rather you have done yourself wrong in entertaining a suspicion unworthy of your generous nature. I am sorry it was necessary to show you that letter.'

'So am I,' she answered, frankly, 'yet it makes me happy to have seen it. It shows me that at one time, at all events, dear papa had quite relinquished his opposition.'

'At one time, yes; and observe, he guards himself against any possible recurrence of his prejudices against me; perhaps they did recur.'

She moved her head in grave assent.

'There you see he absolutely foresaw what might happen to him through weakness of mind.'

Clare did not answer this; she was recalling her last interview with her father on the day of his death, when, although in

a state of extreme physical prostration, his
mind had certainly shown no sign of weakness.   'You will be unhappy with that
man,' he had said, when all his arguments
had failed to move her.

' It is very, very strange,' mused Clare.

' That is what you said when you mis-
trusted my word before I had brought you
the proof of my veracity.   You do not
doubt me now, Clare ?'

' No,' she answered slowly, 'I do not
doubt you now.'

' Well, that is something.   But it will
not be easy to forget that you did doubt
me.   Give me the letter.'

' Why ?'   She put back his extended
hand, and clasped the letter close.

' Because it is hateful to me.   Not in itself, of course, but because whenever I look
upon it, it reminds me of a humiliation.'

' Then you mean to destroy it ?'

' I do.   It is my own letter, though I
have permitted you to read it.'

' Quite true. You can do as you like with it to-morrow, but you must let me keep it to-day, Percy.'

' Very good. I must ask you to remember, however, that it is a private communication. I have forgiven your doubt of me, but I cannot permit others to become cognisant of that insult. It seems that you have already hinted of your incredulity; that was not fair, nor kind, nor like yourself, Clare.'

' If I have hinted of my incredulity, Percy,' she answered firmly, ' I did you a wrong which must be remedied. You spoke just now of "evil counsels" and " detractors." You have none such here; you yourself do me wrong in supposing it. But it is true that I took counsel with an old friend.'

' With Herbert !' exclaimed Percy vehemently. ' He is a prig, and like all prigs a backbiter.'

' That is not true, Percy,' said Clare

gravely. 'You are also mistaken in your
suspicions. I never spoke to my cousin on
this matter. I spoke of it, however, to
Miss Darrell.'

'A born mischief-maker.'

His tone was quiet, but it was easy to
recognise the rage that lay beneath it.
Clare had once or twice before noticed this
in Percy; that he was easily moved to
wrath, but showed great power of self-
restraint. It had seemed to her in him a
proof of good principle and of a well-
regulated mind. But for the first time
there was something in his face that frightened her—a pent-up passion that appeared
to be hot so much restrained as biding its
time.

'No, Percy. You misjudge Miss Darrell,' she answered. 'Moreover, so far
from being your detractor, as it happens,
she took your side. It was I who expressed my doubts of your word, and she
who combated them. In justice to her

as well as you, I will show her this letter, which proves me to have been in the wrong.'

'Very good, my dear ; though for my own part I have no wish to have my character rehabilitated in any eyes save your own. You must promise me, moreover,' he added, after a brief pause, 'for the reason I have already given, that the letter shall be shown to no one else.'

'You may depend on that ; and you shall have it again to-morrow morning. I do not wonder at you setting such store by it, Percy. How good it was of dear papa to write it.'

'Yes, and so like him ; it is not every one who is so careful to acknowledge himself in the wrong, or even to admit he has altered his opinion.'

Clare answered nothing. Her eyes, full of tender tears, were once more fixed upon the letter. It seemed to her as she read it that she was listening to the voice of the dead man.

'It must be clear to you whither all this tends, my darling,' continued Percy; 'there can now be no sort of reason, indeed there never was a reason, but there is now no ground for even a sentimental objection to your naming the day for our marriage. Just now I will not press it, for I can read where your thoughts are ; but when I come to-morrow——'

She looked up at him and smiled. It was the first smile of true love, unmingled with hesitation or regret, that she had given him since her father's death. He folded her in his arms and kissed her, and she returned his kiss.

> 'A lover will not tread a cowslip on the head,
> Though he should dance from eve to peep of day,'

sings the poet. Mr. Percy Fibbert was not a lover of this stamp, but he left Oak Lodge that day with a light step and a light heart. This sort of happiness is wont to communicate itself to others, and on meeting Gerald at the mill that morning (with whom in private he had now some-what stern relations), he gave him a cheer-ful greeting.

On the same afternoon, in an upper room fitted up as a laboratory at Coal-borough Junction, a young man, who had taken but half the dinner hour for his midday meal, was employing the other half in extricating carbonic acid from caustic soda, when a telegram was brought to him by a porter :

To	*From*
Herbert Newton,	Miss Darrell,
Coalborough.	Stokeville.

Come at once, but do not say you were sent for.

CHAPTER XXVI.

THE snow had fallen lightly about Stokeville for many days of frost, and though the town itself was, of course, as black as ever, its environs looked like a landscape out of the Black and White Exhibition, while the neighbourhood of Oak Lodge, which had not more than half-a-dozen tall chimneys within a mile of it, resembled a table-cloth, though it must be confessed one in an economical household, and upon a Saturday night. The gravel-sweep of the house in particular was nearly spotless, and 'threw up,' quite artistically, the red breasts of the robins

that congregated there as usual for Clare's
appearance after luncheon with her crumbs.
After she had fed them and retired upstairs
to her boudoir, which, as we remember,
looked in the other direction towards the
garden, Miss Darrell hopped out like a
robin of another colour, and with a quick,
birdlike glance to left and right, to make
sure she was unobserved, betook herself
into the little shrubbery that intervened
between the road and the carriage drive.

The path was dry and sheltered, and
what was more natural than that the active
little lady should take a few turns there
up and down by herself. Her object,
however, could hardly be a mere 'con-
stitutional,' to judge by the eager way in
which she listened to every hoof and foot-
step on the iron road without, and when
they came nearer stood on her toes and
grazed the tip of her nose against the wall
in futile efforts to look over it. If she had
but been forty years younger, the impatient

vehemence with which she repeated the
ejaculation, ' Drat the boy, why don't he
come ?' would have convinced you she
was keeping an assignation.   Yet ' the
boy ' was doing his best to meet her wishes,
and if not on the wings of love was flying
towards her as quickly as the Coalborough
afternoon express could bring him.   Presently a vehicle stopped some fifty yards
short of the gate where, as she knew, there
was nothing but a milestone to attract the
passenger; and 'regardless of grammar' the
ex-schoolmistress exclaimed, ' That's him.'

She understood at once that Herbert had
stopped short of his destination for the
same reason which had induced her to anticipate his arrival.

' Upon my word,' she cried, as she ran
out to meet him, ' I feel like one of my
own naughty girls — when I *had* girls—
doing something on the sly ; it's quite a
comfort to find a respectable young man
like you descending to the same arts.'

' Well, really,' expostulated Herbert, ' since your telegram said, " Don't say that you were sent for," I naturally took every precaution, and in case you might want to see me alone——'

' Quite right, quite right ; not a word of apology,' interrupted the old lady. ' It is very important that I should have a few words with you in private, and I'm here to do it. Give me your arm—you needn't be afraid of my asking for your hand—and take a turn with me. Herbert Newton, it's a crisis.'

' With Clare ?'

' Of course, with Clare. If it had been anything to do with Gerald, I should have said a catastrophe. It is my opinion she is going to marry Mr. Fibber immediately.'

' Good heavens ! I mean that was nothing more than was to be expected. It was never anything else but a question of time.'

' Perhaps of money, too,' suggested the old lady, tentatively.

' No. To do Percy justice, money had nothing to do with it.'

' You think, then, he really loves her ?'

' He would marry her whether she were rich or poor,' answered the other evasively.

' Aye ; at all hazards. That is just the point. You know how she delayed and hesitated on account of her father's objections to the match. Well, they have been removed in a very singular manner.'

' Removed ? You mean weakened ; that must have happened sooner or later.'

' I mean what I say—removed. Some time before his death, it seems Mr. Lyster had a private interview with Percy, in which, as he tells Clare, her father withdrew his opposition to the match.'

' That is not true.'

' My dear young man, how can you possibly tell that ?'

' I *can* tell it. I am sure of it. I knew

my uncle so well. We often talked upon
this subject, though not, to be sure, very
lately ; but I am quite confident that up to
the very last he maintained his old opinion
of Percy. His fears for Clare's future
happiness never left him, though his
anxiety for her on another account was
still greater.'

'Then you think Percy invented the
conversation in question ?'

'I am convinced that it never took place
so far as Mr. Lyster's being reconciled to
the idea of the marriage was concerned.
He never was reconciled to it. Clare
knows it.'

'She thought she knew it ; but Percy
has persuaded her to the contrary, not by
his assertions, which, truth to say, she did
not credit, but by the corroboration of the
statement in Mr. Lyster's own hand. He
wrote Percy a letter to the same effect as
he had spoken with him, and adding to his
consent his blessing.'

' Impossible.'

' I have read the letter with my own eyes.'

' Show it to me.'

' I cannot do that. Percy made her promise to show it to no one but herself.'

' Ah !'

' You think he had some reason for that. Well, you shall hear what Mr. Lyster wrote,' and she drew from her pocket a paper.

' If Clare said it was not to be read, I cannot read it,' said Herbert gravely.

' She did not say that. On the contrary, she said she wished everybody to know the contents of it, only it was not to be shown. This is a copy of it I made myself from memory.'

' What, word for word ?'

' Certainly. Do you suppose it is only mathematicians who can remember things? You may have logic and reason, which we women have not. I never knew a woman yet who could do a rule-of-three sum—that is, a double one with many terms in it—though of course we taught it ; arithmetic and the use of the globes, etc. ; but I have not given out dictation for twenty years for nothing. I can spout whole pages from " Enfield's Speaker." I read the letter twice, and as soon as I got to my desk wrote out the whole of it; and I can guarantee every word. There is no need for you to look at it—listen.'

As they walked along the raised footpath the schoolmistress repeated to him the letter with sharp distinctness—every word was carried by the keen frosty air into the other's ear. ' Well,' she said, when she had done, and after a long pause, ' what do you think of it ?'

' I don't know what to think. Give me time.'

' There is not much time to spare, and in these matters things strike one at once or not at all. Of course it is a most serious

matter. I hardly dare, even to you, to
suggest the possibility of what is nevertheless in both our minds. Percy said to Clare
" How like" it was of her father so to write.
Is that your opinion ?'

' If he had written at all he would probably have written like that. But it was
not like him to write at all.'

' That is what, I think, struck Clare. It
struck me, too, that it was strange Percy
should have made such an observation. If
the letter was Mr. Lyster's, why should
Percy say it was like him.'

' I don't see much in that,' said Herbert,
thoughtfully.

' Of course it is unfortunate I cannot
show you the original. I am not sufficiently acquainted with Mr. Lyster's handwriting to identify it with any certainty.'

' Clare can identify it.'

' True. There spoke man's inexorable
logic : a woman in your case would have
shut her eyes to that fact: *I* did. It is

possible, however, that the idea of forgery —especially from such a source—never entered into poor Clare's head.'

'No doubt ; but on the other hand she would have dwelt on the handwriting for other reasons.'

'Ratiocination again ; I saw her kiss the letter.'

'You omitted to read me the date.'

'It is December the 8th.'

'What ! Are you quite sure ?'

'Certain. It was on the seventh that he had the interview with your uncle, and on the next day, as Percy affirms, Mr. Lyster put the result of it—that is, reiterated his consent—in writing.'

'Did you see the envelope in which the letter came addressed to Percy ?'

'There was none.'

'No. Nor was there a letter. Miss Darrell, it is a forgery.'

'Great heavens ! Take care what you are saying, sir.'

'If I see the envelope, with the post-
mark December the 7th or 8th upon it, I
will retract the assertion ; otherwise my
conviction remains unshaken. On the 7th
December, as Percy says, he had his interview with my uncle ; that proves the date
for me, which I also recollect, because I
wrote some letters for him that day at his
dictation, one, amongst others, to Mr.
Roden. I say on the previous afternoon, and in my presence, Mr. Lyster
lamed his hand, which caused me to
act as his amanuensis. The wound remained unhealed for many days, nor do I
believe he ever wrote a letter afterwards.
On that day or that night it was simply
impossible that he should have done
so.'

'Will Clare remember this ?'

'No doubt ; she keeps a diary, wherein
I feel certain such an occurrence, since it
happened to her father, will be found set
down.'

'My dear Herbert, this is very terrible. Poor Clare! Poor Clare!'

They had turned back as if by mutual consent, and were walking slowly towards the Lodge.

'Why did you say " Poor Clare"?' inquired Herbert presently, in low, grave tones.

'Because I must tell her this. Do you think it is pleasant for a young woman to discover that her bridegroom is a forger?'

'If you tell her, Percy will never be her bridegroom.'

'You think so,' returned the old lady, with a smile that had a touch of contempt in it. 'It is clear you have never been in love yourself.'

She looked up at him sharply as she said this, and noticed that a quick flush came into his face, and that he kept his eyes fixed upon the ground.

'To be sure you may have been; I forgot you were a man. When a girl loves, the knowledge that her lover is a scamp only makes her pity him. In some cases she loves him all the more for it.'

'Not Clare,' answered Herbert gently.

The old lady looked at him again, but this time out of the corners of her eyes.

'You have studied your cousin's character, it seems.'

'I know her well enough to know that to tell her this will go nigh to kill her.'

'Then it is your opinion that I had better say nothing about it? Yet surely, since we are both agreed that Mr. Percy Fibbert will not make the best of husbands, or, to speak the plain truth, will make a very bad one, it is our duty to save her from him if we can. Why don't you speak, Herbert? Have you no advice to offer?'

'Only that you should do what is best for Clare,' was the quiet reply.

'That was loyally spoken,' exclaimed the old lady admiringly. 'I must think over the matter myself, and it is one in which it is just as well you should not appear. I have got out of you all I wanted, and much more than I expected. You had better go back again to your Junction; work is a good thing for all of us, and is just now the very best thing for you. I'll keep you informed, too, of what happens here; but in the meantime, as the father of one of my pupils—he was a builder—once practically expressed it, work "like a navvy at a barrow." I have found it a panacea for all troubles.'

He shook hands with her warmly, and they parted without another word. 'There goes what I call a wonder,' murmured the old lady, looking after him : 'a young man who is actually not thinking of himself. What powers of abstraction he must have! Poor Clare! Blind Clare! Never has such a half-hour been before me as awaits me now since I had to tell Lady St. Ermengarde that her daughter Evelina Vittoria had run away with our French music-master. Fortunately he was a Count in his own country, which her ladyship found an immense mitigation. But in this case there is no *per contra.* For one's lover to be a fibber is bad enough, but to be a forger! How shall I ever tell it ?'

With trembling limbs and beating heart, but with a resolution as steady as a rock, Miss Darrell repaired to the boudoir. Clare, however, was not there, but in her dressing-room, at the door of which the old lady knocked gently, at the same time announcing her presence.

'Come in, dear Nannie,' said Clare. Her voice, the other noticed, had quite changed within the last few hours. It had regained its old cheerfulness of tone. Her face, too, though pale, had recovered its youth and brightness. She had, for the first time since her father's death, some white in the dress she had just put on, and was in the act of putting a white camellia in her hair as her old friend entered.

'It is not vanity, as you think, Nannie,' she said, smiling, 'that makes me stand before this pier-glass; but my hair is still so short it is difficult to stick anything in it except a comb. Percy said, " Let me see my flower in your hair to-night when I come to dinner," so I am beginning my lesson of obedience. Is it not a beautiful flower? Why, Nannie, what's the matter?'

'Come here, darling: sit by me on the sofa, and I'll tell you what I have to say, though my heart shall break with the shame of it.'

'" The shame of it "? Oh, Nannie, what has poor Gerald done?'

'It is not Gerald.'

Clare turned as white as the flower in her hair, and though her face was fixed and searching as that of the Sphinx, Miss Darrell felt her tremble like an aspen. 'She guesses the worst at once,' was the old lady's reflection, 'which shows the poor dear has her doubts of him. It will be the easier for her to bear it.'

'My darling, I have a sad story to disclose indeed; and it is better that it should tell itself. May I look at your diary?' The little book was lying on the table close beside her.

Clare nodded assent; she could not speak; there was something rising in her throat that choked her.

'I will turn to December 6th. Yes, here it is, just as I anticipated. "Dear papa much the same, but hurt his hand badly in falling against the mantelpiece. Herbert is fortunately with us, who writes all his letters for him." "December 7th. Dear papa visibly weaker. His wounded hand troubles him sorely."'

'What has all this to do with your bad news, Nannie?'

'A good deal, my darling; only too much, alas! Now look at the letter Percy gave you to-day.'

Clare drew it mechanically from her bosom.

'Look at the date, my child.'

'It is December 8th.'

'On which day your father was in-
capacitated from writing.'

'Then there must be some mistake in
the date.'

'No mistake is possible. Your father's
words, or rather the words that pretend to
be his, are, "I have nothing more to say
than I said yesterday morning." That is
the day of his interview with Percy, which
was December 7th. The letter is a forgery;
I suspected it from the first.'

There was a little plaintive cry that
struck the heartstrings, and then all was
silent. Across the beautiful face swept one
look of agony, and then it grew suddenly
still and colourless as death. Clare had
fainted away.

The schoolmistress had had much experience in faints, and knew what was to be
done. While applying the proper remedy,
she did not omit to take the camellia from

Clare's shapely head and put it in a drawer. She had half a mind to destroy the letter itself, but fortunately restrained the impulse.

In a little time the patient's consciousness returned.

'Spare him, Nannie, for my sake,' were her first words ; 'keep his shame secret.'

'No one shall know it who does not know it now, darling,' answered the other softly. The evasiveness of her reply was unnoticed. The expression of the young girl's face, though intensely sorrowful, was far from stern. There was pity, if not love, in it still. Miss Darrell said to herself, 'She will forgive him even this.'

'It is four o'clock, darling,' said she gently. 'What is to be done? He will be here at five.'

'He? Oh no, neither to-day nor ever again.'

'Shall I write to him?'

'No; *I* will.'

'Do not do anything rash. It is possible

—just possible—that Percy may have some explanation to offer.'

Clare shook her head.

'It is all over; he is guilty.'

She rose up, walked with a firm step to her desk, and began to write. Presently she put her hand to her head and looked round, as if in search of the flower she had placed there.

'Here is your camellia, darling.'

'It is not mine; it is his.'

She folded it in the letter, and placed it in the envelope.

'Be sure this is put in his own hand, Nannie. Now please to leave me a little. Do not fear; I am not going to fret.'

Pale as a moonbeam, but with not a trace of tears in her eyes, Clare joined her friend at dinner that evening. Fortunately, Gerald was not present. A few commonplace words passed between the two women, and the girl retained her self-possession even when a note was handed

to her by the servant, which she put in
her pocket without reading. But Miss
Darrell observed that Clare had once more
resumed her deep mourning ; and rightly
guessed that it had the same significance
with respect to Percy as the putting on by
a judge of his black cap. The offender
had been convicted, sentenced, and to
Clare was henceforth dead.

CHAPTER XXVII.

WHEN men, or at least most men, find they have been deceived in her whom they would have made one with them, they cut her out of their hearts as cleanly, if not as easily, as they cut others out of their wills. It is done by one stroke, which is in fact struck by the offender, who is self-erased in the Japanese fashion. The effect is often serious in other respects; some men become jaundiced in consequence, and take to woman-hating or, what is worse, are piqued and propose on the instant to their cook ; but, so far as the once beloved object is concerned, she exists

no longer, or rather is resolved into a case
of mistaken identity.

> 'She is not the ball-room belle,
> But only Mrs. Something Rogers.'

But with women these things are different. When their beloved goes utterly
wrong, they either cling to him and 'go
under' in his bad company, or, if they
have the courage and wisdom to cast him
off, they are consumed with wild regrets ;
they do not easily or soon forget that the
mad dog, whose bite is death, was once
their pet.   He is dead to them, it is true ;
but the effigy of him—not more resembling
him than stuffed animals usually do re-
semble their originals, but in this case a
very complimentary likeness—remains in
their minds' eyes for ever so long.

That Percy Fibbert was a mad dog,
dangerous to the community, and fatal indeed to whomsoever he should be coupled
with, Clare in her heart was well convinced.

Her letter to him, though grave and decisive enough, and affording him no *locus penitentiæ* if guilty, had given him a loophole for explanation ; but he had made no attempt to take advantage of it. His reply had been short, almost offensive. As she appeared to doubt his word, he said, which he was not in the habit of having called in question, he quite agreed with her that it was better they should part company.

'It is a hard letter,' observed Miss Darrell, to whom Clare showed the communication in question; 'but it confirms everything. There is no longer any room for doubt.'

She privately thought it vulgar and even 'maid-servantish;' but she readily forgave its style since its sharpness would probably help to sever the last strands of the bond that bound him to Clare. It did sever them beyond the possibility of reinstatement, and so completely that it gave her

no pang to feel that Mildred could now
have her wish. If there had been need
for it she could have sincerely said that
she owed her no ill-will, and hoped that
Percy would treat her with a confidence
and candour that he had denied to herself.
But though she had exiled him from her
heart, she could not get him out of her
mind. The idea of meeting him, though
in a manner ever so casual and momentary,
was terrible to her, and she kept herself
close prisoner within her own doors from
the apprehension of it.

After a week or two of this seclusion, of
which Miss Darrell easily guessed the true
reason, the energetic old lady took matters
into her own hands. ' My dear,' she said,
' you are getting hipped, and so am I. We
both want change. What do you say to going
to Sandford-on-Sea—for a little while ?'
She added the last words diplomatically,
for her intention was, having once got
Clare away, to keep her there.

Clare had her objections to make; one was that since her cousin was to start for America so soon it would be cruel to leave him.

'It might be cruel if he was bedridden,' was Miss Darrell's dry rejoinder; 'but since the express from Coalborough reaches Sandford in two hours, and as the seaside is at least as pleasant a place for him to pass his leisure-hours in as Stokeville, I don't see the strength of that argument.'

'Then there is Gerald. It would be wrong to leave him to his own devices. This house is dull for him, no doubt'—this in excuse for the fact that he was hardly ever in it till it was time to go to bed, and when he did come showed that he was bored to extremity—'but it still affords him a home.'

'He can be with us at Sandford, and come to and fro by train to business like anybody else, I suppose. Moreover, he is much less likely to get into mischief there

than here. Objection No. 2 " quashed," my
dear, as the lawyers say ; though why not
"squashed" I could never understand, especially as it is longer.'

'You may take me where you like,
Nannie,' sighed Clare wearily. And in
twenty-four hours they were at the seaside.

Why the young heiress did not go to
Blackpool, which is the Brighton of that
part of the world, instead of that 'dead-
alive' place Sandford, astonished many of
her young friends. There seems a general
opinion that after a great trouble there is
nothing like an esplanade with a brass band
on it for restoring serenity of mind ; whereas
unpopulated spots which have only natural
beauties to recommend them are avoided as
having a tendency to promote suicide.

It must be conceded that, even in summer
time, Sandford-on-Sea is not a place that
gives itself up to excitement; while in
spring-time it can hardly be said to awaken
from its winter sleep at all. In this respect,

though sweet enough, it is less like a violet in that season than the 'mossy stone,' which the poet describes as half-hiding it from the eye. It is built of stone, and very well built. It has several good hotels; one of them, 'the Grand,' is about the size of the Langham, Portland-place, and at the period of which we speak had two people in it. It has several fine terraces. It has the prettiest public garden in England. The cliffs are not steep, but to give the idea that they are precipitous, a hydraulic lift is provided, which brings tired pedestrians to the summit for a penny a head. There is a pier, which may be said to be unrivalled, for there is no end to it. The end was carried away by an enterprising steamer under the false pretence of landing passengers, and has never been replaced. The air is divine, and if it had not been so would no doubt have been imported; for the railway company which made Sandford-on-Sea spared no expense. Where they

failed was in making people come to it.
You can bring horses to water (though you
can't make them drink), but it is difficult to
bring society even so far as the seaside unless they have a mind to go there. Perhaps
it would have been some satisfaction to the
railway company—in default of dividends—
if they could have known how thoroughly
Sandford and its quiet suited Clare and her
friend. They established themselves in a
pleasant hotel upon the cliff top, and passed
their time in quiet serenity, save on the
occasions when Gerald honoured them with
his company. He did not hesitate to tell
them that he found Sandford excessively
'slow,' and though all was done for him
that could be done to meet his views—he
had champagne twice a day—he yawned
even over his cigar.

During his first two visits he never mentioned Percy's name; but when he came
the third time he informed them during
dinner that the Fibberts were gone to

London. 'For the season, I suppose?' observed Miss Darrell drily.

'Not they; Lor' bless you, Sir Peter don't care for seasons. He will be there for only a day or two, worse luck to him; but Percy will stay over the Derby, I'll bet a guinea. As for Miss Mildred, she'll stop a month at least, I reckon, for she's gone after her trousseau.'

There was fortunately a vase of flowers in the centre of the table which hid Clare's face from Gerald; her cheek turned pale, and her knife and fork trembled in her fingers. Her heart was beating hard; 'so soon, so soon,' it seemed to say.

'When the wedding is to come off is not, however, settled,' he continued. 'It is said Master Frank is not in a hurry to surrender his liberty—and quite right, too.'

'You mean Mr. Frank Farrer?' observed Miss Darrell.

'Well, of course; who else should I mean?'

The remark was not unnatural, for by
this time Mildred's engagement was well
known in Stokeville. Miss Darrell, however, had only heard of it as a rumour, and
though Clare knew that it was anticipated,
she had felt convinced in her own mind
that Mildred, whom she knew to be at
once passionate and resolute, finding Percy
free, would have found means to break off
with her other flame. She felt it somehow
a relief, though she did not grudge Percy
to Mildred, that that match was not to be.

Gerald had never much appetite, making
up for his deficiency in that respect by what
a certain lady of my acquaintance—she is a
monthly nurse—terms 'drinkitite.' On this
particular evening he ate less than usual, but
consumed a second bottle of champagne.
He was much too well seasoned, however,
to be affected by it ; it only gave him a
'fillip,' as he called it, of which, as it
happened, he stood in particular need.
After dinner he lit a large cigar and

strolled out as usual; but instead of lounging in the street, or dropping in at a certain public-house which he was wont to patronise in the little town, he sauntered out upon the sand.

There was no moon, and the interminable sea looked vaster from its vagueness; at his feet the shoreward wave creamed over with a gentle murmur. He was alone with his thoughts, and that monotonous whisper chimed in with them strangely. 'Better not, better not,' it seemed to say in long-drawn sighs. It was curious how the sound disconcerted him. 'Curse the sea,' he muttered under his breath; and finding a cliff path after some difficulty, ascended it, and began to pace to and fro on the moorland without the town. The lights of the houses were only dimly visible, but to eastward there was a large and steady light, which reddened all the air about it. He knew that this was from the great iron-foundry miles

away, the furnaces of which burned like
the sacred fire of Vesta, night and day con-
tinually; but to-night they wore a mystic
and uncanny look he had never seen in them
before. The voice of the sea could hardly
have reached him there, but the words
' Better not, better not,' recurred to him with
persistence, and he seemed to read them
as on a placard, huge and black against
that distant glare. He felt in his pocket
for a brandy flask he now always carried,
and took a deep draught; but even that
failed to compose his nerves or warm the
blood in his veins. His nerves were utterly unstrung, and he knew it. ' I am not
myself,' he said aloud, with angry vehemence, as though he were apologising to
himself for some mental weakness. It
would have been well for the unhappy boy
if he could have changed places with anybody else. It was not till after a second,
and even a third application to the flask,
that he could bring his wits to bear with

any steadiness on the matter in his mind,
and even then he occupied himself (as the
wicked are wont to do) with the result of
what he was proposing, rather than with
the plan itself.

'It is a large sum,' he murmured, 'and
all to be paid on the nail. And then I
shall get away from all this and away from
him.' Here followed a frightful execration. 'With that money no doubt I could
do well enough by myself—but Rachel? I
must give her the slip, or all's lost. To
think that a man like me should have tied
such a millstone around his neck with his
own hands.' Here followed more 'cursory
remarks,' as highly coloured as those which
had preceded them, but this time directed
against himself. 'What a fool, an ass, a
dolt, I was to be so cajoled and jockeyed!
The vanity of that slut has been my ruin.
Not that she has much to boast of now,' he
added, with a bitter smile. 'Well, I'll get
quit of her as soon as may be, somehow or

another. Gad ! I don't know whether I
don't hate this other one as much. Three
hundred a year. Yah ! I detest such
meanness. What is it to me that Oldcastle says this, and Oldcastle says that ;
it is not enough, nor half enough. She
gave me fifty pounds last week, it is true ;
but what's fifty pounds to one with her
income ? What do I care for her promises
of what she will do for me when I come of
age ; when I marry (*when* I marry ; the
fool of a girl little guesses !) or when I set
up in business for myself. I want it *done.*
And since you won't do it for me, my
pretty little minx, it shall be done for me
by somebody else at your expense. Yes ;
the present value of what I am to have for
this little job will be more than all such
expectations put together. And then I am
to get away, clean away, beyond seas.
That's the plan—*his* plan—and a very
good plan too—that is, unless one hits
upon a better. It will be well worth her

while to square matters, then I can cut the
painter just the same with twice the coin
in my pocket and leave him raging, which
will be worth half as much again. It is
true I there miss Herbert, whom the other
scheme will ruin; he has no security for
his money, and of course when she finds
herself in want of it she'll stick to it. I
should like to ruin Herbert. But there,
one can't have everything. It was not so
wise of you, Master Percy, as you thought,
to take yourself off to town, while I was
making a clean breast of it. By the time
you come back again, if Clare is wise, I
shall be a thousand miles from Stokeville.
Whichever way it turns out, nothing but
good can come of it, that's certain. She
will never let the thing be made public, for
the old man's sake. Percy's right there;
I'm safe enough from judge and jury.
Still, I would give something if the next
half hour or so was over. It's a nuisance,
too, that she has that little old woman with

her. They are at their coffee now. If
you're stubborn, Miss Clare, you may have
to come down to chicory. Oldcastle told
Herbert the other night that that bank
had stopped. It's lucky they're not here,
though I shall have to meet 'em before
all's well. There's a whisper, too, that Sir
Peter's been over-trading ; as it happens
that don't matter either way ; but I hope
it's true. I should like to see Miss Mildred's nose, that is so high in the air,
brought down to the grindstone. How I
hate everybody !'

He had finished the flask by this time,
and was frank and natural. It is a common error to suppose that scoundrels are
not scoundrels in their own eyes, but on the
whole have rather a good opinion of themselves than otherwise ; and that, even in
the privacy of their own self-communings,
they gloss over their viler sentiments and
pay lip service to virtue. As a matter of
fact they do nothing of the kind, only

while acknowledging their atrocities they excuse them as being done in retaliation for certain wrongs inflicted upon them by mankind in general, which in truth are the misfortunes begotten by their own misdoings. The 'Implacable, Unmerciful,' so justly denounced in the Scripture, have (unless they are quite desperate) very tender feelings with respect to their particular case, and though their hand is against every man, are exceedingly indignant when a finger is raised, even in reprobation, against themselves.

The task that lay before Gerald Lyster involved as he well knew (though it must be conceded that he underrated it in common with all moral pains) the infliction of excessive distress upon an innocent person; yet that idea did not so much as enter his mind, nor, if it had done so, would it in any wise have disturbed his equanimity; on the contrary, since the person in question had offended him, it would have presented

itself to him in the light of a retribution,
and even of a judicial punishment; as
matters were, he thought only of his own
part in the affair—how he should demean
himself, how most easily persuade, and
how escape from unpleasant consequences.
The man who can say ' No' as agreeably
to himself as saying ' Yes,' has his counter-
part in the scoundrel who has surmounted
scruple, and the attribute in each case
ensures success—not, however, without
some drawbacks.

It was the custom with Clare and her
friend to retire together early, leaving
Gerald, by no means unwilling, to his
own devices; but as they lit their candles
on the night in question, Gerald said in a
hushed, grave tone, ' I should like to have
five minutes' conversation with you, Clare,'
whereupon Miss Darrell withdrew with a
pleasant ' I shall see you presently, my
dear,' designed to keep up Clare's spirits,
and also, perhaps, to remind her that she

had an adviser, without whose counsel it would be well not to compromise herself.

Miss Darrell had not a good opinion of Gerald Lyster, but it was Heaven high in comparison with what it would have been could she have guessed what was coming.

CHAPTER XXVIII.

THE WITNESS.

'WHAT is it, Gerald? For heaven's sake, speak!'

In his nervous agitation the young man was drumming on the table with one hand and stroking the down upon his lip with the other; his eyes were downcast; his face was pale to the lips, which twitched incessantly. 'It is bad news, very bad news,' he murmured. That was clear to her without his saying it; he looked a messenger of evil tidings from head to foot; his endeavour to counterfeit sympathy, as if resented by the muscles of his face, which had never been put to that work before, gave him the air of a moulting raven. 'Not bad for me,' he added, gulping something in his throat, 'but bad for you.'

Here he expected Clare to shriek out, or perhaps to faint, instead of which, to his amazement, her face assumed an unequivocal appearance of relief. 'It is not shame, then,' she said to herself, 'whatever has happened.' Then immediately afterwards she exclaimed, 'I hope nothing has happened to Herbert.'

'Not that I know of,' returned Gerald petulantly; the idea of her thinking that anything relating to her cousin could have moved him so aroused his contempt, which was unfortunate, since the impression he wished to convey was that of a wounded spirit.

'Sit down,' said Clare, 'and tell me all. I am not so unused to misfortune but that I can bear to hear your news, whatever it is, Gerald.'

'It is not news so far as I am concerned,'

he began, with his eyes on the carpet. ' I
have known it ever since our father's death,
only I did not like to speak of it. It
was wrong of me, but I kept silent for
your sake.'

'That was a mistaken kindness, Gerald;
never mind, go on.'

'I dare say you have observed, Clare,
how down in the mouth I have been for
this long time; how out of sorts and unlike
myself. Well, as you will soon learn, there
was reason enough for it. Can you carry
your mind back to the night of father's
death?'

'Most certainly.' Indeed, she might
have added, 'My mind is seldom elsewhere,'
but instinct told her that any such assertion would be out of place.

'Well, I was upstairs, you know, while
you and Percy and Herbert were below.'

' My father wished it to be so—that is, so
far as we were concerned,' she answered
quietly.

'Just so; but as for me, I was too miserable to eat anything.'

'I remember you left the table soon after dinner,' said Clare coldly.

On all other matters she extenuated Gerald's shortcomings, but this pretence of his having felt a more poignant sorrow than herself for the dying man offended her and stung her into plain speaking.

'Well, at all events, I was upstairs when no one else was. I was in my own room, full of sorrowful thoughts, when I heard a noise next door—that is, in my father's room. I stole in on tiptoe, and this is what I saw.'

He hesitated and stopped; his tongue felt dry and his lips parched; and in the silence he heard once more that warning murmur from the sea—' Better not, better not.'

'I saw my father, who had crept out of bed and dragged himself to the mantelpiece, putting back the hand of the clock.

He had put it back a few minutes or so
when some noise—perhaps he had heard
my footsteps—attracted his attention, and
he turned and climbed into his bed again.
I was so amazed that I did not move for a
moment or two, and then, hearing nothing,
I grew frightened and went in to father,
and he looked so white and strange that I
called you up—as you must well remember
—only just in time to see him die.'

'This is a very strange story,' said
Clare, gravely, looking at her half-brother
intently, who, however, kept his face
averted from her, 'nor do I understand
why you have hitherto concealed it.'

'To spare you,' he murmured hoarsely.

She shook her head.

'If it was so, I thank you. That such
a spectacle should be most distressing I
can easily believe; but since you did not
mention its occurrence at the time, why
mention it now?'

'I couldn't help it; my conscience

pricked me so. I have not had a happy moment since, and I was obliged to relieve my mind, no matter what should be the consequences. I am very sorry, for your sake.'

'What do you mean ?'

'Is it possible,' he answered, stealing a glance of amazement at her, and then reverting to his old dogged look, 'that you don't see what hangs on this. It was those few minutes which did it—which established your claim to be in the partnership for another year.'

She had not seen it until it was thus pointed out to her; the question that had so monopolised her father's thoughts, aggrieved Sir Peter, filled Percy with hopes and fears, agitated the whole world of Stokeville, had occupied but a very small space in her mind; now, however, everything was made plain to her as by a flash of lurid and ghastly lightning which leaves all dark behind it.

She rose from her chair and confronted Gerald.

'Do you dare to say then—you, his son —that our father, finding himself about to die, used his last breath to defraud some fellow creature of his rights ? You *liar.*'

Gerald shrank into his chair like one who has received a blow, and cowered there as though expecting another.

'No,' he murmured, 'I don't say that.'

'What *do* you say, then ?' Her eyes flashed fire, but her voice was ice-cold with disdain.

'I say,' answered Gerald doggedly, 'that the old man was mad ; that through always wondering whether he should live over the year or not, and through dwelling upon the consequences, he got his brain into a morbid state, and just at last, like one in his sleep, not knowing what he did, but as it were mechanically, he put his wish —the father to the thought, you know— into action. That's my view of it.'

If it was so, it was only a view he had
very recently—in point of fact within the
last minute or two—taken into his consideration. It had been his intention to suggest
the very thing which had provoked this
storm; but his sister's manner had frightened him. Familiar though he was with
duplicity, he did know sincerity by sight.
He felt that it was not self-interest that
had provoked Clare to express disbelief in
his statement, but her confidence in her
father's innocence. Upon that point he
was convinced that she was capable of op-
posing his testimony to the uttermost, and
in the presence of all the judges in the land.
So, on the spur of the moment, he had hit
upon this idea of 'unconscious impulse' to
explain matters, which at once left his own
statement where it was, and relieved his
father from the imputation of wrongdoing.

'It is very strange,' said Clare, regarding
him thoughtfully and with great intentness.

'Of course it is—I mean *was;* nothing

could be queerer. He had to crawl along
the floor, poor old man, to get to the fire-
place. I don't blame you for denying it—
nobody could believe it who hadn't seen it.'

'Still less could any one who knew him,'
answered Clare thoughtfully, 'believe that
he could do such a thing in his right mind.' ·

'Quite right,' said Gerald ; 'that is what
I have kept saying to myself all along.
And since he didn't do it on purpose, and
since nobody could ever dream of his having
done such a thing at all, it of course remains
a question for your consideration whether
it is worth while to tell anybody about it.'

'You mean about the actual fact,' observed Clare gravely.

'Just so,' he answered, glancing at her
for the second time, in hopes to read her
thoughts. He began to hope from her last
words that things were turning out in the
best manner possible, namely, that while
believing in his statement she would agree
to keep it secret. He knew, as we are

aware, what it was to receive hush money; and though he had had an all too short experience of the sensation, it had been very sweet. In this case, since he could trust himself to drive a good bargain, he would obtain a fortune, and with it what was equally desirable — his freedom. If Clare's case had been his own, he would, of course, have made terms at once; and though he did not give her credit for such good sense, he hoped that was what it was coming to.

'As our father was unconscious of what he did, Clare, there is really nothing wrong in the matter.'

'There is not a shadow of wrong,' answered Clare confidently.

Now this was going a little too far for Gerald. It was very prompt and judicious of her to take this sensible view of the transaction, but if she was really going to persuade herself that she might be silent without scruple, where would be his hold

upon her ? It was high time for him to
hint that what he had seen was not only
strange as she had called it, and a very
curious instance of mental phenomena, but
valuable otherwise than as a contribution
to physiology, namely—to the spectator.

'Well, when you say " not a shadow of
wrong," Clare, in which I cordially agree
with you, you must remember that that may
not be the view of the outside public, who
did not know our father as we did.'

'That is just what I am thinking about,'
replied Clare simply.

'In the eyes of mere casuists, in fact,'
continued Gerald, 'it may be doubtful
whether our father's act, though unconscious, may not seem to have the same
effect as though it had been done de-
signedly.'

'Good heavens! Do you suppose I am
thinking of keeping the money ?'

Gerald stared at her aghast. He was
all at sea again. If she was not thinking

of keeping the money, what on earth was she thinking of?

'Well, you said, yourself,' he answered doggedly, 'that it would not be necessary to reveal the actual fact.'

'I meant, sir—that we never need speak of what—you *say*—you saw.'

He was still ignorant of her meaning, but he dared not put another question to her; that 'you say' of hers convinced him that she still harboured doubts of his main story.

'It is very easy,' she went on, 'to convince some people that money belongs to them. Let Sir Peter have his dues; he will not be particular to inquire into how he came by them.'

'Oh, if you really mean to throw up your chance,' said Gerald, 'that part of the business will be easy enough. Sir Peter is always going about saying how hard it was that he should have lost his money by five minutes; if you choose to have conscientious scruples about it being such a narrow shave, he'll share them, I warrant; he'll take all he can get, and only look on it as restitution.'

'Let him look on it how he likes, in Heaven's name,' ejaculated Clare, 'so long as our father's memory is kept stainless. You and I well know that it is as pure as snow, and in that, although we lose our all, he will still have left us a rich legacy.'

'Well, as for me,' said Gerald, in an aggrieved tone, 'I am not aware that he ever left me anything else worth speaking of. The whole matter is one for your own consideration, not mine. You seem still to doubt my story, but what reason can I have for inventing it ? You don't suppose I'm in Sir Peter's pay, do you ? In so far as the thing affects me at all I shall lose by it, for I suppose that beggarly three hundred a year, to which Mr. Oldcastle persuaded you to limit my allowance, will go with the rest.'

' To be sure ; I had forgotten that,' sighed
Clare, 'and my good intentions are gone
with it; we shall both be losers by our
honesty, my poor Gerald.'

'Good intentions ? What do you mean,
Clare ?' inquired the other excitedly.

'Oh! no matter. It can make no difference now. And yet I should like you to
know that I was not so hard upon you as you
persuaded yourself to think I was. On the
day you came of age half the money, the
loss of which you regretted so, would have
been settled on you.'

' But look here, in that case I have a
contingent interest in this matter,' interrupted Gerald. 'You must not do anything
in a hurry and without consultation with
me. Why the deuce didn't you tell me
about all this before?'

' It is better as it is, Gerald,' she answered with a sad smile : 'you have been
saved from what might have been a
terrible temptation ; though I hope you

would have revealed everything just the same.'

'I hope I should not have been such an unspeakable idiot,' exclaimed Gerald naïvely. 'You don't really mean to say that you are going to throw away your money—*my* money—for a mere caprice ?'

'A caprice ! It is an act of common honesty. Would you have your father's daughter be a thief, brother ?'

Gerald looked at her as Claudio might have regarded Isabella. He murmured something about her conduct being quixotic, but attempted no further argument. He saw the mischief was done as regarded those contingent expectations of his, of which he had only heard when he had lost them, and cursed what he deliberately termed his 'folly.'

'Of course I would wish you to do nothing wrong, Clare,' he answered complainingly ; 'it is very hard that you should always misjudge me so. As to what you suggest about concealing the actual facts, I think . you are most judicious; nobody need know about them save you and me.'

'Nay, some people must know about them, Gerald : it is only right that I should repay the confidence which others have placed in me by taking counsel of them.'

'Counsel ? I don't know any good that you have done to yourself or anybody else' (he was thinking of Mr. Oldcastle's advice, which had restricted his allowance so meanly) 'by taking advice of that sort. I should have thought your nearest relative —myself—would have been the proper person to advise with. Of course you will do as you please; but people will talk, however much they have shown you confidence, as you call it, and if once the story gets abroad I wonder how many will believe that the governor did not put on the clock on purpose—I mean in his right mind ?'

'I see that quite clearly, Gerald,' she

answered gravely; 'there is danger on
every side.'

'And on one side certain ruin, Clare,
remember that.'

It was his last shot fired in desperation.
If it went home, as it could scarcely fail of
doing, it would surely give her pause.

'It will make us very poor, no doubt,
Gerald,' she answered gravely; 'but it will
at least leave us honest. Do not suppose
that I feel angry with you for having done
your duty; quite otherwise. I am grateful
to you for having preserved me from com-
mitting an unconscious wrong. Of course
it is a bad thing for both of us in one way;
but the having relieved your mind of such
a burden must of itself be grateful to you,
and a time will come—the same that came
to our dear father—when you will rejoice
in what now seems loss as a great gain.
Think, think, Gerald, that perchance he is
now cognisant of what we do, hearing perhaps the very words we are now saying!'

'Oh Lord,' interrupted Gerald, pushing back his chair, 'I wish you wouldn't talk like that! I hate it. I thought we had come to Sandford to keep our spirits up.'

'Does it distress you to talk about the dead, Gerald?' she answered gently, almost pityingly. 'Well, well, I will say no more. I will now go to my own room, and think of all you have told me, and what is best to be done. Good night, dear boy.'

She stooped down and kissed him. He did not move his face to meet hers, but sat with shut lips and a frowning brow, the very image of moody discontent. He could not have better played his part (though he acted naturally enough) in the plan he had in view. His demeanour went far to remove any lingering doubts she might have entertained of the truth of his tale. He looked exactly as a man might have been expected to look who, having confessed something to his own detriment, repents of his frankness. But in reality his heart

was full of fear as well as of chagrin. That
Clare believed his story was now clear
enough, but would those others, whom she
had expressed her intention of consulting,
believe it? She herself was ready enough
to give up her share in the profits of Fibbert
and Lyster, but would she be permitted to
do so without investigation?

That notion of his father being cognisant
of all that had just passed affected Gerald
more than he could have thought possible.
Of course it was all 'rot,' but it was a very
unpleasant idea to lie down with on one's
solitary bed at night. He had a brandy and
soda, and another cigar before he retired, to
help him to get rid of the notion; but even
those remedies failed to restore his equanimity. Moreover, happening to look out
of his bedroom window, which faced the
great furnace fires, a still more unpleasant
thought suggested itself. The words,
' Better not, better not,' were no longer to
be read in them, but the flame now re-

minded him of a certain old picture he had
been attracted to as a child in Sir Peter's
mansion, depicting in the ancient material
way the place of lost souls. Something
whispered to him as he gazed at its lurid
glow, ' If hell has but one man in it, that
man will be Gerald Lyster.' The notion
was egotistic. He might easily have pictured to himself at least one companion,
but even had he done so, that would have
afforded him anything but comfort.

CHAPTER XXIX.

EVERY mature mind is aware that
when two ladies are alone together
at night, with their brushes in their hands
and their back-hair down, that is the
supreme moment for the reposal of confidence. Miss Darrell had not much to
brush, which enabled her to give her un-
divided attention to her young companion,
who retailed to her all that Gerald had told
her without hesitation or reservation. Miss
Darrell had passed the age of astonishment,
but just at first her brush dropped upon her
knees; and as if that action had mechanically affected her muscles, mouth and eyes

flew open to their extreme limit. As Clare proceeded, however, she gradually recovered herself, and by the time the narrative was concluded, could have recited the whole prospectus of her scholastic establishment without a mistake—her test for her intellect being in full marching order.

' Well, my dear, my conviction is that your first impression concerning the matter is the correct one. I believe the whole story to be a falsehood from beginning to end.'

' What! Do you really · think that Gerald is so wicked as to have invented it ?'

' I don't know about "wicked," my dear, though some men—aye, and women—are more desperately wicked than you have any idea of ; and I don't say a word about invention, for I have no high opinion of your half-brother in that way ; but that he has told you a deliberate lie I have small doubt.'

'But what motive could he possibly have in thus defaming my father's memory? He never loved him, but there was no quarrel between them; and even if there had been, surely no human being—let alone the case of father and son—would carry his enmity beyond the grave?'

'It is often done, Clare, nevertheless,' sighed the old lady; 'but I readily acquit Gerald of any such intention. He is not that kind of person.'

'Moreover,' continued Clare, 'he can get nothing by it; nay, he loses a certain income which—though, as it happens, it falls short of his expectations—is surely worth having.'

'There, of course, is the difficulty,' mused the old lady.

'Unhappily, he does not like me, Nannie, and persists in misunderstanding me, who have no other wish than to do what is most kind for his own good; but even if he hated me, he would surely not wish to compass my ruin, in which, moreover, he himself is involved.'

'He did not know that,' put in the old lady quietly; 'but, nevertheless, I am so far of your opinion. Gerald would not do you any harm unless he could do himself good by it. The question is, Is there any-one else who has a grudge against you, and who in gratifying it would at the same time benefit himself?'

'My dear Nannie, how can you talk so! I have not, thank heaven, an enemy in the world.'

'I did not say "an enemy;" I said one who had a grudge against you. Think, think.'

'You cannot mean Percy?'

'I did not mention him, but since you have done so, I may say that it is not only women who resent being cast off by those whom they have loved.'

'Oh, Nannie! one might regret it and even resent it, but surely, surely, one could never wilfully injure one whom we have once loved!'

'My dear Clare, you could never wilfully injure anybody. Yet, undoubtedly, there are many people who have no hesitation in doing so. Your own feelings, therefore, go for nothing in pursuing an inquiry of this kind. We are dealing with natures that are altogether out of your experience. I have known scores of them. It is quite possible that Percy Fibbert has a grudge against you; he has good cause, or cause that he may call good, for having one. It is no use your denying it' (for Clare held up a remonstrating hand). 'I know that man well, and he is one neither to forgive nor to forget. Granted, then, that he would willingly—or, as you term it, wilfully —do you an injury, the next question is, Has he anything to gain in the present case?'

'What can he have to gain by injuring poor me?'

'Well, I don't know how much, of course,'. pursued the imperturbable old lady ; 'but if you turn out to be disentitled to any share in the profits of the firm, the other partners are proportionately benefited by it.   Percy is a partner, is he not ? Mr. Oldcastle told me that Sir Peter's expectations of this year's gains were something enormous.'

'But what has all this to do with Gerald's story, Nannie ?'

'In my opinion a great deal.   Perhaps Percy and Gerald have formed a limited company of their own, to which Percy contributes the invention.   Gerald does not possess that faculty.'

'Do you mean that they have entered into a conspiracy together to commit a fraud !'

The old lady nodded, shut her eyes, and pressed her lips together. She might have sat for a miniature monument of Conviction.

'But even supposing anything so wicked could have entered into Percy's mind, why should Gerald join in it? He does not like Percy.'

'No; that is one great advantage of disliking everybody: in some cases, at all events, one must be right. Gerald, as you say, dislikes Percy, but he is very much afraid of Percy. Some people are like wild beasts, with whom love does nothing and fear everything. The whip cracks, and Gerald jumps through the hoop. That is my solution of the enigma.'

'A very far-fetched one, dear Nannie, in my opinion,' answered Clare sadly; 'and one which I should be very very sorry to believe myself.'

'As to its being far-fetched, my dear, I don't see how you could expect to find it nearer,' said the old lady, with a momentary display of 'temper.' She plumed herself, not without some reason, upon her knowledge of human nature (though in this case,

perhaps, her prejudices, at least as much as
her sagacity, had led her to her conclusion),
and she resented having it called in question. The next moment the sight of Clare's
pained face banished from her bosom every
feeling but tenderness. 'You speak of
being sorry to believe such things, my darling; there was a time when I was sorry
too, even for those who commit them. I
keep my little stock of sympathy now for
the victims only. Do you not think I have
some for you? Clare, Clare, my darling,
child of my dead friend! you have been
cruelly deceived, infamously plotted against,
but you shall not be wronged if I can help
it. I will write to an honest lawyer whom
I know this very night; Mr. Oldcastle is as
honest, it is true, but he is not so keen.'

'What!' interrupted Clare; 'write to a
stranger, to reveal what, if that which you
believe is true, must be my brother's shame!
Or worse, to one who, since he did not know
my father, may impute fraud to *him!* Oh

no, oh no! As Gerald says, if once the
thing gets abroad, the world will be sure to
think my father guilty.'

' He said *that*, did he ?' interrupted the
old lady ; ' do you suppose he cares about
your father's memory ?   Not he.   Depend
upon it, he has reasons of his own for avoid-
ing publicity.'

' And I, Nannie, have not I the reason
which you suggest he only pretends to
have ?' continued Clare firmly.   ' True or
false, no earthly consideration—nothing,
nothing—will induce me to permit this story
to become the subject of public discussion.'

' Do you mean to say,' exclaimed the
schoolmistress, with indignant severity,
' that you will submit to be robbed by a
footpad rather than call for help to the
passers-by ?   Nay, that is a feeble image
for the position you are taking up.   Will
you permit yourself to be reduced to ruin
by two scoundrels ?'

'Nannie, dear Nannie, pray spare me!' expostulated Clare entreatingly. 'In speaking so harshly, and, as I honestly believe, so unjustly of the persons in question, I might well say you do your own nature a grievous wrong; but since such an argument may have no weight with you——'

'Not a feather's,' put in the old lady coolly.

'Then I appeal to you for my own sake. Every injurious word you apply to Gerald and—and—to Percy, is a stab to me; I do not believe them guilty. For the moment, it is true, I was inclined—I know not why —to come over to your opinion.'

'Instinct,' observed Miss Darrell remorselessly.

'No, no,' she pleaded passionately; 'it is instinct that repels such base suspicions. With all his faults Gerald could never have devised so foul a plot, and in a manner so cruel. Strange as it is, I feel his story must be a true one. I suppose

if I give up my claim, it will be necessary
for Mr. Oldcastle to know it ?'

'He is one of your trustees, that's all,'
put in her companion drily.

'True; and Uncle Roden is another.
It would be dreadful to have to discuss the
matter with Uncle Roden,' said Clare, with
a shiver.

'I am sure he would treat you with
great consideration, because he would
believe you to be a lunatic.'

'Oh, Nannie, do not be hard upon me.'

'I am not hard, Clare ; but it makes me
mad to see you so hard upon yourself. As
if the villains of the world did not prosper
sufficiently without innocence and simplicity
playing into their hands. It is a cruel wish,
but oh that I could lend you my own
bitter experience for the next few days !'

'One must act according to one's lights,'
said Clare gently.

'In knowledge of the world, my dear,
yours are as a farthing candle. That's very

rude, of course, and I apologise. I'm in
such a state of irritation (not with *you*, my
darling ; I have nothing but pity for you),
but with the monst—that is, with the world
in general, that I am not in a fit state of
mind to give advice. Go to bed now, and,
if you can, to sleep. In the clear dawn of
morning more reasonable thoughts will
come to you. At present you are con-
fronting a nightmare.'

Clare rose with a smile, and embraced
her old friend affectionately. How different it was when they had last wished
one another 'good-night'! It seemed to
her, by comparison with her present condition, that she had then been crowned with
content, without having deserved or being
grateful for it. And now ; now!

Certainly in some respects the wisest of
human creatures are, ah! those whom we are
in the habit of considering the most foolish;
who catch the fleeting pleasure as it flies,
and, while the sun shines, bask in it; who

have few apprehensions and less regrets ; and who, if they never rise to the heights of human happiness, find easy footing on the tableland of it, and by some beneficent law of their nature never gravitate to the depths of human misery.   To such as these the death of a father is 'the common lot,' and the loss of a lover an ephemeral cala- mity, while the anguish that was now op- pressing Clare was simply an impossibility. For what Miss Darrell was feeling for her —the probability of her being stripped of means, and exposed to the untempered winds of poverty—she felt not at all.   Her terrors were immaterial, and shook the very soul within her.   On the one hand, she trembled lest the finger of public scorn should be pointed against the memory she revered above all earthly things ; on the other hand, she shrank from the suspicion that her father's son had committed an un- paralleled and inexpiable baseness.

' " I do not believe them guilty," were her

words,' mused Miss Darrell, as through the
night she paced her room in her dressing-
gown and slippers, or flung herself impa-
tiently into her arm-chair, because the
counsel she demanded of her own quick
wits was slow to come. 'She said so, but
she does not believe it, nevertheless. And
yet she will let them have their way rather
than risk exposure. Fortunately Herbert
is coming to-morrow morning, and he will
see Gerald face to face.'

A reflection that had so soothing an effect
upon the old lady that, towards morning,
she retired to bed and slept a little.

CHAPTER XXX.

NOTWITHSTANDING their bad night—for Clare had not been so fortunate as her friend, and had snatched no wink of sleep—the two ladies met at breakfast at the usual hour. Clare, self-involved in her own sad thoughts, took little note of external objects, but Miss Darrell's quick eyes perceived that the table was laid for two only.

'Gerald is gone,' she said; 'I ought to have anticipated that.'

'Why so? Perhaps the waiter has forgotten him.'

'It is much more likely he has forgotten

the waiter,' returned the old lady, acidly.
She considered Gerald mean in all ways,
and no longer thought it necessary to withhold her opinion.

The man was summoned, and at once
informed them that 'the young gentleman '
had departed by the six o'clock train to
Stokeville, where he said he had very particular business. ' He told me to give this
note to you, miss,' addressing Clare.

She did not open it till the servant had
left the room, when, having read it, she
handed it to her companion without com-
ment.

' I am obliged to be early at the mill this
morning. All that I told you last night is
true from beginning to end.'

' Nevertheless,' observed the old lady,
scornfully, ' it does not bear daylight. He
was afraid of being tackled by even me,
you see.'

It was a modest observation, for the fire

in the old lady's eyes and the vigour in her
tone would not have recommended her
just then to any adversary as one to be
easily ' tackled.'

' How glad I am,' she continued, ' that
Herbert is coming by the first train this
morning.   I think I shall go and meet him.'

This was artfully put, for if she had
said, ' Shall we go ?' Clare could hardly
have declined, and it was Miss Darrell's
wish to see Herbert alone before he saw
Clare.   He had seen Clare once, and once
only, since her engagement with Percy had
been broken off ; and on that occasion no
allusion had been made to it.   It was a
delicate subject between them, because he
had known Percy all along, and had
warned her against him until matters had
gone too far for warning.   And though
she knew he would never have dreamt of
saying ' Was I not right ?' or ' Did I not
tell you so ?' Clare had somewhat shrunk
from meeting him.

The happiness Herbert felt for her escape
was easily concealed, since compassion for
her misery overwhelmed it; but, nevertheless, feeling that he had no sympathy
with her previous infatuation, and that
Clare knew it, he too had been glad when
that interview was over. But now—now
that he was coming to see her for the second
time, a free woman, with a future before
her, his heart beat high within him, and not
only with the thought of her enfranchise-
ment. He had always loved her dearer
than any human being, but so long as he
could remember — though she had been
always kind and even affectionate to him —
another had been always preferred before
him. He knew little of women's ways, and
it seemed inexplicable to him that his uncle
should have detected his love while its
object had remained in ignorance of it.
The greatest pleasure the old man had had
in those later days had been to talk of
Clare to Herbert; to praise her, to dwell

35—2

upon her sweetness, her unselfishness, her
helpfulness to himself and all about her;
and his greatest misery (though it had a
morbid attraction for him) to bewail her
shortsightedness and her mistaken choice.
And though he never spoke of it directly,
he had given Herbert to understand, not
only that he would have preferred him of
all men for a son-in-law, but that he had
divined, had not Percy stood in the way,
that the desire of the young man's heart
would have been to stand in that relation.
For a man of science Herbert was modest
even about his professional acquirements;
and in social matters had a very humble
opinion of himself. With young women of
his own class he knew that he was at a disadvantage; it was as difficult for him to
interest himself in croquet and lawn tennis,
in their gossip about society and their
anecdotes of the aristocracy, as for them to
sympathise with his aspirations to guide a
balloon, or his ambition to walk about

under water ; he hated afternoon teas and balls, and small talk, in which, indeed, Clare herself took little pleasure ; and his incapacity to appreciate them gave him a sense of difference from other men of his age, and, therefore, of inferiority. So far from thinking himself too clever, he ascribed his want of appreciation to some serious deficiency in his own nature, and bewailed it as one might regret the want of an ear for music.

In a general way he was conscious that this handicapped him very heavily in his efforts to get on in society; that in a girl like Mildred Fibbert it excited indeed something like contempt, while even with Clare he must needs cut a very poor figure in comparison with a man like Percy. But now Percy was gone, certain vague hopes which had hitherto been kept down by the weight of circumstances began to arise within him and take shape. Clare was different from other girls. When she had

come to see him on one occasion at the
Junction, and found him in his working
clothes, she had not been horrified, or
even amazed (as Mr. Roden had been),
and would have shaken hands with him,
notwithstanding her delicate gloves, if he
would have permitted her. He had shown
her over the works, and she had taken an
intelligent interest in all he had to tell her,
and put pertinent questions to him about
this and that, which had contrasted very
favourably with those of other visitors.
She had expressed a genuine sorrow at
his proposed departure from England; he
had postponed it for her father's sake, but
since the old man's death mail after mail
had started for South America without
him. Why? He had persuaded himself
that he had been waiting for Clare's
marriage; but that ceremony would certainly have had anything but an attraction
for him. If he had asked himself why he
was waiting, he could have given no

definite, and certainly no satisfactory
reply. That Clare had a very sincere
regard for him, he knew; he had been
told by Miss Darrell that her young
friend 'respected him very highly,' but he
was not quite sure that that sort of estima-
tion was to his advantage in his present
case. Women 'respected' their parish
clergymen, their family solicitors, their
uncles by marriage, but such a feeling
seemed somewhat to preclude a more
tender sentiment. There was indeed one
undoubted point in his favour: his suit
would be backed by Clare's knowledge of
her father's love for him. To have to
rely on the good word of a dead man for
one's success with a young woman is not,
however, very encouraging; and Herbert's
modesty represented it to him as his main
chance; but there were two things at all
events which his professional education
had taught him—the exceeding value of

Patience and Perseverance and the danger
of ' Haste, half-sister to Delay.'

As he drew near to Sandford his spirits
rose. The morning was brilliant and the
' numberless smile' of the sea seemed to
reflect itself on his own features. He had
promised himself, at Clare's request, what
was very rare with him, a few days of complete holiday, and here was an Eden to
spend it in, not without its Eve. Perhaps,
as she had written in her invitation that
there was nothing to be done in the place,
and he must expect dulness (the idea of
dulness where Clare was !), she might
come to meet him at the station. He
scarcely thought of Miss Darrell, which
was very ungrateful of him, but took it for
granted that she would come with her.
And there she was on the platform looking
out for him eagerly enough. He looked to
right and left for her companion, and even
when he was shaking hands with ' the old
lady, glanced about him inquiringly.

Clare is not here, Herbert,' she said, gravely. 'She would have come, but something has happened.'

'Good heavens! No accident! She is not ill?'

'No; she is well enough. Send your luggage on to the hotel, and give me a few minutes' talk before you see her.'

His heart beat very fast; he had a vague notion she was about to make some communication to him respecting his cousin of a tender kind. He knew Miss Darrell had a kindness for him, and perhaps was about to confirm his hopes, though he had never whispered of them. Women, he had read, were so quick-sighted in such matters.

Who of us has not been similarly fooled by Fate; been certain that she had this or that wished-for gift in her hand, and lo, when it opens, there is nothing, or the very thing in all the world we least desire? It is fair to add, though the fact, as it happens, has no place here, that often when that same Fate seems frowning, and has her fist doubled as if for a blow, her features suddenly relax with a smile, the fingers open, and out comes the unexpected gift.

Miss Darrell led the way across the road into the public garden, in which no public ever entered, because there was none. A ravine by nature, a paradise by art; through the midst of it, far down, ran a small stream, which, to the upper terraces, sent only a gentle murmur; from the walks jutted here and there little promontories, from which the most charming views were visible, and on each of these coigns of vantage was a rustic bench. On one of these they seated themselves. In spite of the tumult of his mind, Herbert, who had never been at Sandford before, or dreamt that so much beauty could lie so near Stokeville, could not restrain his admiration.

' How very very beautiful!' he exclaimed.

' Yes,' said his companion, drily, ' but as

often happens when the earth is so fair
there are serpents about ;' and then she
told him Gerald's story. He interrupted
her occasionally with a remark very much
to the purpose, but otherwise listened with
great calmness. There were no indignant
outbursts such as she had expected; his face
grew a little more ' set,' as is the way with
thoughtful faces when those who wear them
are deeply moved ; and once or twice he bit
his lip, but that was all.

' You do not seem surprised ?' she said
when her narrative was concluded. ' You
have surely heard nothing of this before ?'

' No, nothing; but then,' he added signi-
ficantly, ' I know Gerald.'

' Then you must feel that this story of
his is a falsehood ?'

' I should have known that even if I had
not known him. I was at Oak Lodge that
night. And as we sat at supper—a miserable pretence of a meal, but so my poor
uncle would have it—I remember just before

we were called up to him, the town clock striking midnight.'

'Just before.   Are you sure of that?'

'Quite sure.   I remarked upon it to poor Clare, and she said, "I can't think how I came to miss hearing it, for I seem to do nothing else but listen."   Those were her very words.'

'It is strange you should have remembered them so accurately,' observed Miss Darrell, glancing at him curiously.

'I remember all she said and all she did, both then and afterwards,' answered Herbert simply.

'Then this testimony of yours and hers settles the matter.   Mr. Lyster did survive into the New Year.'

'Unfortunately we were not disinterested witnesses,' observed Herbert, gravely.

'To be sure, I forgot that you were in the firm yourself.'

'I have no legal position in the firm

whatever,' he said ; 'you are quite mistaken.'

'I don't mean as partner, but you have
money in it——'

'There seems to be some misconception
about that,' interrupted Herbert ; 'Mr.
Oldcastle, however, knows all about it.
When I said " not disinterested," I referred
to my relationship to Clare, and the possibility of my uncle leaving me something,
which, as it happened, he didn't do.'

'I am quite sure you never thought of
that,' said the old lady, confidently.

'I 'am thinking of what other people
will think, my dear Miss Darrell.'

'When one knows one is saying truth,
sir, and doing right, that ought not to
matter twopence halfpenny.'

'So far as I am concerned,' said Herbert
smiling, 'you may deduct the twopence.
But what people will think—and say—
about this, will matter to Clare very much.
You and I know she would not tell a false-

hood to save her life ; but it is only natural,
or at least excusable, that people who do
not know her should attribute an interested
motive for her making the statement of
which we speak.'

'Do you imagine that any jury in the world
not composed of convicts would disbelieve
Clare's evidence as opposed to Gerald's ?'
exclaimed Miss Darrell, vehemently; 'why,
he has "hang-dog" written all over him.'

'This matter will never come before a
jury,' answered Herbert, sadly. 'Nothing,
nothing, I am quite sure, will ever induce
Clare to permit it to become the subject of
public discussion.'

'Her very words,' murmured Miss
Darrell to herself; 'he knows her every
thought, poor fellow,' and she looked at the
young man with that tender sympathy
which women over fifty can still feel ;
among men, to be sure, judges retain the
faculty of shedding tears even beyond that
epoch, but it is only when for the nonce

they have become feminine by putting on a
· cap.

'But Herbert, you and Clare were not
alone that night.'

'True; there was a third person who
heard the clock strike, or, at all events,
heard my remark upon it.'

'Percy Fibbert?'

'Yes.'

'Well, surely his testimony would be
disinterested enough, and if he makes the
least pretence to be an honest man he will
give it.   Then, even if Gerald's story were
true, there would be no sort of good in his
repeating it.'

'But there would be a good deal of
harm,' answered Herbert, gravely.   'It is
the story—that is to say the disclosure of
it—and not the fact that Clare fears.'

'Herbert Newton, let us be frank with
one another,' said the old lady, earnestly;
'Percy could stop all this if he liked.'

'I have not the slightest doubt of it.'

'But you don't think he will stop it ?
Yet we should be asking no favour of him
in urging that, but only the barest justice.'

'What would Sir Peter say, Miss
Darrell, if his nephew's testimony pre-
vented Clare's share of this year's profits
from passing into his hands ?'

'Good heavens, what has that to do
with the matter, I mean with Percy's
telling the truth ?'

'Morally, nothing of course ; but I am
putting myself as far as I can into Percy's
shoes.'

'You'll never get your toes into them,'
exclaimed the old lady vehemently. 'That
man is a rascal.'

'And yet you are taking it for granted
that he will voluntarily give up the claim
which Gerald's story would establish for
him.'

'We will try, at all events,' said the old
lady.

'I am doubtful about that,' resumed

Herbert, thoughtfully. ' I think you should take counsel with wiser heads than mine before hazarding such a step. Remember, his reply, so far as Clare is concerned, will be final; and it is not from Clare such an appeal can come. Her trustees should be consulted.'

' I have telegraphed for both of them this very morning,' said the old lady, though the notion even of telling *them* about this matter was most distasteful to her. ' If I had not been here I do believe she would have given up everything without a struggle on Gerald's bare word. Here is the note he left behind him :

' " All that I told you last night is true from beginning to end." '

' " Methinks he doth protest too much," ' quoted Herbert, drily.

' Protest! Yes, indeed; I think, however, I should have got the truth out of him if he had stayed here. My fear is that he will tell his tale to somebody before we can get at him; if he has not told it already.'

'If somebody else has not told it to him,' observed Herbert.

'Ah! then you think as I do,' said the old lady quickly, 'that this story, like those of Erckmann-Chatrian, is collaborated.'

'Stop,' said the young man firmly; 'I entreat you to say no more. I am not a fit person to discuss what you have in your thoughts. I was picturing to myself certain effects which disappointment and dislike might give rise to in the mind of another, without taking into consideration how they might move—nay, how they do move— my own. I am not a fair judge in this matter.'

'Well, I don't understand you. You were frank enough about Mr. Fibbert's character the other day, when he was only open to the suspicion of forgery; and now, since he has been found guilty and drummed out, as it were, of Clare's affections, you won't open your mouth against him. I do hope you will not be so reticent when she herself asks your opinion upon this matter.'

'She will never ask my opinion about Percy Fibbert,' he answered earnestly; 'and as for me, unless she does ask it, my mouth is sealed.'

'Who sealed it?' asked the old lady sharply.

'Clare herself.'

'Indeed!' exclaimed Miss Darrell, looking up at him with wistful curiosity. 'Lately?'

'No; months ago. I promised her never to say a word against him.'

'Oh, well! I must say,' exclaimed the lady bitterly, 'it is difficult to act with people so ridiculously full of scruples as you and Clare. It is like having for allies some very worthy comrades, but who insist on bringing their wives and children into battle with them. Let me tell you, my good friend, we have to contend against foes who have no such ties.'

' Nevertheless, what is right will come uppermost, and justice be done,' observed Herbert confidently.

' It is possible,' answered the old lady drily ; ' but, like Napoleon, I prefer to have on my side strong battalions. So, by your leave, we will not discuss this matter with Clare till my reserves come up.'

' You mean till Mr. Oldcastle arrives ?'

' Yes, and Mr. Roden. You may smile, my good sir, but I would rather have a child to fight for me, than a man with his hands tied and his mouth sealed. Come, let us go in.'

CHAPTER XXXI.

A RICH individual of my acquaintance who is the architect of his own fortune, and admires the architecture, was once so good as to tell me how he made his money. 'I have no blood, sir, but I have brains; I have no learning, but I have common sense; I have no crest, but I have a motto : it is " Shove ;" ' which he illustrated by an appropriate action—the protrusion of a gigantic shoulder. Yet, when one considers the matter, this excellent principle is not always the talisman of success. There are even some people who get things through *not* shoving ; as though one who watches the surging crowd round a stage-door, but hesitates to take part in the trampling of women and children, should be beckoned in by an appreciative manager through a side entrance, and given a front place in the pit. When this happens the manager is generally a female; but it does happen. I doubt, for example, whether Herbert Newton lost much in the opinion of Miss Darrell, though she expressed herself about it so contemptuously, by declining to speak his mind about Mr. Percy Fibbert. The opportunity of climbing into one's beloved object's good graces by stepping on the prostrate body of a defeated rival offers such a combination of pleasure and profit as is almost irresistible; but a woman—because perhaps she appreciates the temptation so thoroughly — is sometimes capable of appreciating the self-sacrifice of him who declines it.

Clare, who had seen Herbert's portmanteau arrive, guessed easily enough what had delayed him and Miss Darrell. Indeed she had (very improperly) watched from the window their flirtation in the garden.

The old lady, who was judiciousness itself, left the two young people alone together for half a minute.

'She has told you all, Herbert?' said Clare, in a hurried whisper.

' All.'

' Then of Gerald's two alternatives—for one is impossible—does that theory of his that dear papa was the victim of a mechanical impulse seem to you credible?'

' It is as incredible as the other alternative,' said Herbert gravely.

'And that lad is his own son.'

' It is terrible; but he is but a lad, as you say.'

' And therefore open, you would in mercy add, to evil influences.'

' I was not going to add that, Clare; but it is true, no doubt. You once rebuked me for uncharity to him, and reminded me very properly that he and I were of widely different temperaments and dispositions.'

She remembered it very well, and the occasion ; how she had not only defended her half-brother, but some one else ; and, in particular, how Herbert had said that there was one person who had a permanent influence over Gerald, 'the more's the pity.' She knew that Miss Darrell had communicated to Herbert her suspicions of that person's handiwork in the present matter, and she honoured her companion's reticence in forbearing to retail them.

'Oh Herbert—dear Herbert—what are we to do ?'

Miss Darrell entered the room as the question was concluded.

' Nothing,' she answered for him—' nothing at present. Your trustees, my dear, will be here this afternoon—I have received a telegram from each of them—and no decision can be arrived at in their absence.'

It struck her as highly undesirable that

these two young people—one so full of
sentiment and the other of scruples—should
come to any understanding on so weighty
a matter without consultation with their
seniors.

'It is a beautiful day; let us enjoy it, and
forget this trouble till the time comes to
bear it.'

The proposition was full of wisdom, but
difficult of accomplishment. Who of us who
have survived the good old days of school-
time—the days which those only can call
'golden' who are themselves brazen—can
forget that miserable morning of the day
we departed to resume our studies for the
second term, when, though still small, all
illusion was at an end as to what school—
and the boys—were iike. We were still
for a few hours with our parents and our
friends ; no one for the moment was pulling
our hair, or borrowing our money, or stealing our cake ; the kindly atmosphere of
home was yet around us. And yet how

hopeless were all attempts at enjoyment in the shadow of the coming sorrow. There are some people—murderers—who eat the very heartiest breakfast on the morning on which they are to be hanged; but such powers of mental abstraction are exceptional. The probable villainy of her half-brother, the possible baseness of her quondam lover, the disgrace that menaced the memory of her father, these things Clare could not forget even for a moment. They dulled the spring sunshine for her, and tainted the very air. Nevertheless, the sense that she possessed Herbert's sympathy in the matter was of some comfort to her. From those husks of conventional consolation 'well meant for grain' (but which go nigh to choke their unhappy recipients), she was as safe in Miss Darrell's care as in his own; but she knew he could enter into her filial feelings, which the other could not. Every touch of his hand, every tone of his speech, assured her of it.

So far as his influence could effect it, she was convinced that, at whatsoever sacrifice of fortune, the dead man's fair fame would be kept free from stain.

All three went to the station to meet their expected visitors. The London train, which was to bring Mr. Róden, arrived a few minutes before the Stokeville one, by which Mr. Oldcastle was to travel. The former gentleman was in a state of great effusion.

'How very good of you, uncle, to have come so promptly,' exclaimed Clare, with genuine gratitude.

'My dear niece, every trouble undertaken for you—however onerous—is, and always will be, a pleasure to me. Miss Darrell, I am charmed to make the acquaintance of my beloved niece's most devoted friend. And Mr. Hubert, too! Delighted, I am sure, once more to meet you; a most auspicious occasion.'

For the moment Herbert thought him

demented, but Miss Darrell had a shrewd
suspicion of what he had in his mind, and
hurried him off to the hotel, not unwillingly.
It was inconsistent with his dignity to wait
on a railway platform for a country at-
torney, and he had also anxieties about his
luggage.

'I hold it to be a great principle of life,'
he said, 'never to lose sight of one's portmanteau. My good man' (this to the hotel
porter), 'why do you turn it bottom upwards?
You always do it, I know; have you any
logical reason for it?—So my dearest niece
is going to marry her cousin after all.'

'Good heavens! what put that into
your head, Mr. Roden? I was afraid you
would have said something to that effect in
Clare's presence.'

'I, madam? Indeed, you little know
me,' he replied, drawing himself up; 'I
am the discreetest of men. But surely
that is the same young gentleman I once
met under widely different circumstances,

covered with oil. Hubert; I remember the name from " King John." '

' His name is Herbert—Herbert Newton ; but Clare is not going to marry him, nor anyone else.'

' But this is most extraordinary,' complained Mr. Roden. 'Why, what am I brought here for ? I am come down at a vast inconvenience and some expense——'

' The telegram said your journey would be paid, sir !'

' Pardon me, my dear madam; be so good as to permit me to proceed. The journey, as you say, is provided for out of the estate ; but of course there will be extras to which a man in my position can make no allusion. Delicacy forbids. I make no complaint on that score, but surely I have not been inveigled for nothing to this abandoned and deserted spot ? Good heavens ! where are the people ? Is there any infectious disorder from the ravages of which the inhabitants have fled ?'

'My good sir——' expostulated Miss Darrell.

'Once more pardon me, and permit me to conclude,' proceeded Mr. Roden. 'I have in that portmanteau a little cadeau for my sweet Clare. It is of the rarest and most delicate china—great heavens! how he is bumping it round the corner in that handbarrow!—and specially designed for the interesting occasion which I had pictured myself as about to attend.'

'I am sorry to say, Mr. Roden, your presence has been necessitated by quite another matter, and under circumstances far less agreeable. Mr. Oldcastle is coming on the same account.'

'Good gracious!' exclaimed the valetudinarian, adjusting his scarf with a shiver; 'you don't mean to tell me that I have been brought down here in springtime, when east winds are proverbially prevalent, upon a mere matter of business!'

'It is one, however, of some importance,' observed Miss Darrell drily, 'since
it seriously affects your ward's fortune.'

'I hope it does, madam,' answered Mr.
Roden testily; 'that is to say, I hope it
will turn out to be an affair of sufficient
weight to excuse such an extraordinary
proceeding. What on earth can she have
been doing to affect her fortune? Young
girls should never have any money; they
are never satisfied till they have lost it.'

'Very likely; no doubt it is best that
men should have everything,' observed
Miss Darrell, her smothered indignation
finding vent in satire, of which the other
was quite unconscious; 'but, as it happens,
Clare is not to blame in this case. The
misfortune has arisen from the conduct of
her half-brother; you remember that young
man, I dare say?'

'Of course I do. Edgar—Edgar Lyster,
son of Clare's father by his second marriage,' returned Mr. Roden, with some

pride, arising from the consciousness of unwonted exactness.

'Not Edgar—Gerald,' interposed Miss Darrell gently.

'To be sure, as you say, not Edgar. I was thinking of "King Lear." Shakespeare is a passion with me. So they've found out Gerald at last, have they? I read him like a book in those few days I spent at Stokeville. A young fellow, rather loose, or if the expression is too coarse for a lady's ear, let me say "fast," but without any real harm about him; the mere exuberance of youth. Eh, what? Tells falsehoods? Now there you show your discernment, my dear Miss Daredevil —Deverell, I mean. I should say he was a most tremendous and unmitigated—yes —liar.'

'You are right there, Mr. Roden,' exclaimed the old lady with genuine approval; 'whatever Clare says to you, stick to that. This is our hotel. Clare ordered a fire in

your room, as the spring air is chilly; and I
hope you will find everything comfortable.
In ten minutes or so we shall have afternoon tea, if you ever take such a thing.'

'My dear Miss Deverell, you will make
a sybarite of me; no, I don't take tea
before dinner, but I take coffee—*café noir*
—with just a dash of curaçoa in it.
Thanks.'

In the meantime Clare and Herbert had
arrived with Mr. Oldcastle.

'What is the matter?' were the lawyer's
first hurried words as he stepped out of the
train. 'You have had no communication
from the Bank, I do hope?'

'The Bank!' said Clare; 'what Bank?'

'Oh, never mind. I was afraid that
certain persons connected with the—but as
they haven't done it, it doesn't signify—
might have been making some direct application to you, instead of through the
proper channel. It would have been highly
unprofessional, but—well, if it is not that,

it will keep.   I never talk business in the
open air.   There's a text against it.   The
birds of the air will carry the matter.   Mr.
Roden here, did you say ?   What on earth
did you send for him for ?   Important !
That's the very reason why you shouldn't.
Advice !   You might just as well have
called in a Chinese Mandarin.'

The co-trustees, however, shook hands
across the tea-table with much cordiality.

' I am delighted to meet you again, my
dear Mr. Newcastle,' said Mr. Roden, ' and
under more auspicious—or at least, taking
the average, less melancholy circumstances
than on the last occasion.   Let me recommend a little curaçoa in your tea.'

' Not if we have a business matter to
discuss,' said the lawyer, smiling.   ' Now,
my dear Miss Clare, who is to be the
speaker—you, or Herbert, or Miss Darrell ?
Or is it a matter of united testimony ?'

' It certainly is not,' observed Miss Darrell sharply.   ' The story you are about

to hear is utterly destitute of corroboration. Clare, my darling, I am afraid you must repeat to these gentlemen what you have already told to me. I wish I could spare you the task.'

It was certainly a painful ordeal for poor Clare, though she had the sympathy of her whole audience, who did their best to relieve her from embarrassment. Mr. Oldcastle put in a question here and there, which, so far from interfering with the flow of narration, was of great advantage to her, as, in answering his queries, she divested herself of the *rôle* of public speaker. Once Mr. Roden inquired whether there would be any objection—as he found his feelings on his dear niece's account getting a little too much for him—to his smoking a cigarette; but otherwise there were no interruptions.

CHAPTER XXXII.

WHEN Clare had finished, everyone looked towards Mr. Oldcastle, except Mr. Roden. Perhaps that gentleman did not understand that what was required was a professional opinion, and rather resented that this appeal should not have been made to himself as a man of the world, and occupying so high a position in it, in the first instance. At all events he took occasion to make a remark which at once attracted attention to the proper quarter. 'Well, I must say, my dear Clare, that Gerald is deserving of great credit.'

'It is just there that I differ from you,'

replied Mr. Oldcastle, with unwonted promptness. ' Credit is the very last thing I should be inclined to accord to his story.'

' Pardon me. You are too hasty,' continued Mr. Roden, with a pitying smile. ' I was about to add, when you interrupted me, that Gerald deserves great credit for ingenuity ; but that when we had praised the young man's talents for fiction, our admiration was exhausted.'

' What we have first to look to in a statement of this nature,' observed Mr. Oldcastle, ' is motive.'

' Just so,' assented the valetudinarian. ' My dear Mr. Herbert, oblige me with a light—or, since we are dealing with a work of art, should we not use, my dear sir, the French word *motif* ?'

' In plain English, however, which I believe we all speak,' pursued the lawyer grimly, ' the question simply is, What does he get by it ? As I have said, the story

is incredible to me; but it is also inexplicable why Gerald should have invented
it.'

'Not at all,' answered Mr. Roden. 'If
even the young gentleman had said he had
put the clock on himself I should not
attach one whit more importance to his
statement. From a love of notoriety people
often confess to murders they have never
committed ; and as for Master Gerald, he
has already done a good stroke of business
in the way of sensation by bringing us down
here on a fool's errand.'

'There is some truth in what you say,
Mr. Roden,' admitted Miss Darrell ; 'but
you don't know Gerald as we do. There
is not only method but meaning in all he
does. A practical joke is the last thing to
enter his mind.'

'There I quite agree with you, Miss
Darrell,' said the lawyer gravely. 'Indeed,
saving Miss Clare's presence, who has the
misfortune to be related to him, I fear that

the young man has much more knave than
fool in his composition.'

' You have had proof of that, eh ?' put.
in the little lady sharply.

' Why—yes—' (the lawyer was thinking
of that cheque for five-and-twenty pounds,
the circumstances connected with which
Percy had hinted had better not be inquired
into)—' I am afraid I have. Now, my dear
Miss Clare, there is one point in what you
have told us that seems to me of the last
importance : the question would be a painful one for me to put if your character were
not well known to every one of us, but is it
not your impression that at one time, at all
events during the course of Gerald's interview with you, he had the idea of obtaining
hush-money ?'

' He did say,' answered Clare, with a
deep flush, ' that it was a question for my
consideration whether it was worth while
to tell anybody about this matter. He explained that, however, in another way.'

'Just so; he saw he had gone too far,' interrupted the lawyer, 'and then went off on another tack. That course of conduct is very common in such cases. After that plan failed he was less strenuous in his assertions, I conclude.'

'Of the truth of his story? Not at all. Indeed, after the interview was over—the next morning—he left this note behind him :

'"All that I told you last night is true from beginning to end."'

'Then he had two strings to his bow,' remarked the lawyer thoughtfully.

'And a deuced long bow it was,' remarked Mr. Roden.

'Quite right, quite right!' exclaimed Miss Darrell. 'As a matter of fact, Herbert Newton here is a witness to the falsehood of Gerald's statement; he will tell you that the town clock struck midnight before he and the rest were summoned from the

supper-table to Mr. Lyster's room, when
they found him still alive ; so there was
not only no need for fraud on the part of
the dying man—a monstrous idea, to begin
with, to anyone that knew him—but an
absolute impossibility of its commission in
respect of time.'

' That is so,' observed Herbert ; ' I remarked to Clare at supper that night that
the town clock had just struck, and that it
was therefore time to go upstairs, as we had
promised her father to do.'

' And she heard it also ?' put in the
lawyer.

' No, I did not hear it,' said Clare, ' but
was as certain of the fact as though
I had, since Herbert affirmed it. Indeed, it was corroborated by the clock
upstairs.'

' That is, of course, the clock in your
father's room to which Gerald's statement
has reference,' observed the lawyer. ' Miss
Darrell speaks of " the rest ;" there were

others, then, besides you and Newton and Gerald present on that occasion ?'

'Gerald was not there,' said Clare gently ; 'he was upstairs, you know. But there was one other person with us—Mr. Percy Fibbert.'

In his earnestness and satisfaction, Mr. Oldcastle did not remark the hesitation with which this name was mentioned, nor the blush that accompanied it.

'Then that settles the matter. Percy is what you, and indeed Newton, are not ; an independent witness. In fact, his interests lie quite the other way ; and it is not to be conceived but that, as a man of honour——'

Here he stopped, for he suddenly re-membered that the relations between Clare and Percy had been abruptly broken off—for what reason he did not know, but probably a disagreeable one ; perhaps, not finding her so wealthy as he had expected, and notwithstanding his protestations (often made to the lawyer himself) that money would make no difference to him in that matter, he had jilted her. Moreover, the looks of all around him were so peculiar that Mr. Oldcastle felt he was getting on dangerous ground.

Before Miss Darrell, who was about to speak, could get out a word, Mr. Roden, delicately removing his cigarette, observed:

'You may hold any opinion of the gentleman you please, Mr. Oldcastle; but as my dear Clare's nearest relative and trustee I must protest against anything whatever relating to her material interests being left to the honour of Mr. Percy Fibbert.'

'You are a most uncommonly sagacious man,' exclaimed Miss Darrell, with irrepressible admiration.

Mr. Roden bowed, smiled, laid his hand upon his heart, and daintily resumed his occupation. He had no objection to be called sagacious, but the fact was, it was

no knowledge of Mr. Percy's character
that had thus moved him, but the remembrance of a certain evening passed at Sir
Peter's, on which he had been treated with
much less consideration than was his due.
The *amour propre* of much wiser men
than Mr. Roden is at once their strongest
and their weakest point, and any wound
inflicted on it goes to the very root of
what they are pleased to term their
opinions.

Neither Clare nor Herbert uttered a
word, but their silence, as Mr. Oldcastle
felt, was sufficiently significant.

'Perhaps there are some here,' he said,
'who are in possession of other facts concerning this unhappy matter than have
been communicated to me. Is it possible that there is any suspicion of collu-
sion ?'

'I have none, Mr. Oldcastle,' answered
Clare firmly; 'nor are there any grounds,
as I believe, beyond mere prejudice, for

such a suggestion. We have only to
consider Gerald's story in relation to himself, and, what to me is paramount, so far
as it affects the memory of my dear
father.'

'But, my dear Miss Clare, even Gerald
does not presume to suggest any intentional misdoing upon the part of Mr.
Lyster. He said, as I read it in my notes
here, that he performed the action imputed
to him " like one in his sleep," or "under an
unconscious impulse," which your brother
himself explains as having arisen from his
brain being in "a morbid" state through
its constantly dwelling on his chance of
survival into the present year, upon which
such important interests depended. I am
bound to say from my knowledge that
your poor father did give a great deal of
thought to that contingency.'

'Of course, if Gerald's tale be true,' said
Clare, 'such would be the only explanation
of the matter to those who knew my

father. But I am thinking of those who
did not know him. Do you suppose that
money—all the money in the world—
would compensate me for the defilement
of his good name ? No ; at all risks, at any
sacrifice, I will keep it unsullied.'

'My dear Miss Clare,' said the lawyer
gravely, 'I cannot and will not imagine
that your speech implies anything so
monstrous and ruinous as an intention to
give up what the fortunate prolongation of
your father's life has secured to you ; a
competence which he may be truly said to
have earned for you, since Dr. Dickson has
assured me many times that nothing but a
supreme effort of will enabled his patient
to live on as he did; but if such a mad
notion should have taken possession of
you, I must point out that nothing would
be more likely to produce the very. misfortune that you dread, since the giving up
of your undoubted rights would be a tacit
admission that you had no claim to them ;

and if no claim, that it was abrogated by
your father's act.'

'I have thought of all that, Mr. Oldcastle,' returned Clare gently, 'and I
think I have overcome the difficulty, if
Gerald's tale is to be accepted.'

'A large "If,"' ejaculated Miss Darrell.
'One hears of stories of a Cock and Bull,
but they are Gospel to it.'

Mr. Roden emitted a little stream of
smoke in the speaker's direction, as though
it were so much incense, and kissed his
hand in gallant adhesion.

'I say if Gerald's tale should on the
whole be accepted as correct,' pursued
Clare, quite unmoved by these demonstra-
tions, 'I think my plain duty could be performed without the danger to which you
allude. It is certain that only a very few
minutes made the important difference to
my prospects of which you speak; indeed, as
you know, Mr. Oldcastle, I have felt some
scruples (though your arguments over-

came them) in taking advantage of that
circumstance, and why, though late, should
I not once more entertain them ?   The firm
would hardly be very solicitous to inquire
into my reasons for this change of views ;
but if necessary it would be easy to attribute them to what, if (I say again) Gerald's
tale be true, would be the true cause—
namely, that since the event in question we
have discovered that my father's clock, on
the correctness of which everything hinges,
was a few minutes fast.'

'My dear Miss Clare, the case is admirably put, but——' here the lawyer hesitated, smiling blandly, with his fingers on
his watch-chain.

'But you were about to say,' interposed
Miss Darrell, 'that persons suffering
from mental aberration do sometimes put
absurd cases admirably. My dear Clare, I
blush for your intelligence. Mr. Roden,
did you ever hear anything so unreason-
able ?'

'My dear Miss Darrell, let me say rather, unseasonable; it is midsummer madness.'

'Still,' pleaded the lawyer, smiling, 'there is method in it; is there not, Mr. Newton?'

'Indeed, sir,' answered Herbert, 'supposing, as Clare says, we are to accept Gerald's story as true, it seems to me no better plan than hers could possibly be devised for combining restitution with secrecy. I don't think Sir Peter would stir the question of how she came to find the clock fast. I agree with my cousin that it is impossible to exaggerate the importance of Gerald's statement; but I am much more disposed than she is to hold it a complete invention. As he sticks to it, however, of course it must be investigated; and this, because of Clare's delicate but very natural feeling in the matter, is our difficulty. We can only appeal from Gerald drunk, as it were, to Gerald sober; get him to retract a statement which by this time, perhaps, he regrets, if only from fear of the consequences.'

'In plain English,' observed the lawyer, 'we must make it worth his while to tell the truth.'

'I will have no bribery,' exclaimed Clare decisively; 'not one shilling shall be given with my consent to close anyone's mouth.'

'What! Not to prevent this young man telling a falsehood!' exclaimed Mr. Roden, throwing up his dainty hands. 'My dearest Clare, where is your morality?'

'At all events,' observed the lawyer diplomatically, 'there can be no harm in giving Gerald the opportunity of withdrawing his allegations in case he repents of having invented them. He suggests, what we don't think very possible, that his father was actuated, in what he is affirmed to have done, by a mechanical impulse; perhaps Gerald was driven to invent this very singular narration by a similar hallucination.

If he repents his false step he will know that, as has just been said of Sir Peter, we shall not be very solicitous to inquire how he came to make it.'

'My opinion of him, nevertheless,' remarked Miss Darrell, with a tightening of her lips, 'whatever explanation of the phenomenon he may offer, will remain precisely the same.'

'That, however, my dear madam,' replied the lawyer cheerfully, 'such is the callousness of the human heart to moral reprobation, it is probable he will survive. What we are brought here to-day for is to put a stop to a calumny such as, thanks to certain scruples on dear Miss Clare's part—which we will not go so far as to say do greater honour to her heart than her head— may become a calamity; it is only a little spark at present, but if it once spreads there will be a conflagration. What we want is not to bring Gerald to book—for that his accounts will be cooked we may be certain

—but to obtain from him a retractation. I propose, therefore, to write to him in a guarded way, informing him why we have been summoned here, and requesting his immediate attendance, at the same time taking care to afford him not only an opportunity of recantation in case of repentance, but also a loophole of escape.'

'It will be a composition that will require very delicate handling,' observed Mr. Roden drily, 'especially the construction of the loophole.—I am quite of your opinion, my dear madam.'

This last was an aside in reply to a muttered aspiration from Miss Darrell, that the said loophole could be a slip-knot attached to a gallows.

'Oh, as to that,' observed the lawyer, smiling, 'in such cases a mere keyhole is amply sufficient for exit. I hope this plan, my dear Miss Clare, as being fair to every-one, as well as merciful to Gerald himself, commends itself to your sense of right.'

At the moment Clare was thinking of a letter somewhat similar to the one proposed, written of late by herself, and also leaving a loophole, and what came of it. How hard it was to find baseness in one so dear, and now again (for it seemed taken for granted) in one so near!

'I suppose it is the wisest course,' she sighed. 'I thank all here from the bottom of my heart for all the pains they are taking for my sake.'

But she felt, as everyone could perceive who heard her, that it was labour in vain.

CHAPTER XXXIII.

THAT metaphor of Mr. Oldcastle with respect to a conflagration should the spark of calumny once get ahead was by no means an exaggerated one. It was clear to all the little party now assembled at Sandford that should Gerald once communicate his story, whether it was false or true, to other ears, irreparable disaster must needs follow. The proposed letter was therefore despatched to Gerald by the next train to Stokeville, the guard being instructed to place it in the young man's own hand. In it he was adjured by every tie that is supposed to be sacred to retract the charge against his dead father, which, though absolutely incredible to ordinary ears, was making his sister miserable, while at the same time he was assured that, in making a clean breast of it, he would obtain her forgiveness. The simple phrase, ' he would be no loser,' which the lawyer had added in place of the last sentence Clare had struck out with her own hand. ' Just as you please, my dear young lady,' he had said, with a shrewd conviction that the young gentleman would have taken forgiveness in a very material sense. In adding that all that was wanted from him was the truth, Mr. Oldcastle had also pointed out to Gerald that his omission to come at once to Sandford would be a tacit confession that the whole story was an invention. ' My own private impression,' the note concluded, ' is that it was a practical joke, designed, I must say, in the worst taste, but still not of course the unforgivable sin ; and I can only hope you have already repented of it '—which was the loophole.

At Clare's earnest request Mr. Oldcastle ' gave himself a holiday '—a present he seldom got from other people—and stayed the night at Sandford, in hopes that there might be some reply from Gerald by post the next morning. She felt that, next to Herbert, the lawyer understood her best, and could be patient even with what he might consider morbid weakness in her with respect to the matter in hand; whereas, though they would be powerless to move her from any settled purpose of her own, she rather shrank from the sharp antagonism it might evoke from Miss Darrell, and from the contemptuous philosophy of Uncle Roden. As it was, Miss Darrell could not restrain herself from giving utterance to significant opinions with reference to the wickedness of weakness in certain cases ; and how people with the best intentions in the world often did more harm for the sake of peace and quietness, or from sentimental considerations, than the most terrible tyrants. To give way to injustice in one's own case was, she argued, the most certain method of encouraging it in that of others, and, under the guise of self-sacrifice and patient submission, was in effect to act most selfishly and to the disadvantage of the whole human race. To Mr. Roden, for whom she conceived an unwonted admiration from the manner in which he had ' put his foot down ' on Gerald's story, she appealed with confidence for corroboration of these views.

'My dear madam,' he said, ' I have no doubt you're right : conciliaticn in the case of a disagreeable person is not only thrown away, but most injudicious ; it leads him to imagine you are afraid of him, and encourages him to further acts of aggression. At the same time I am bound to confess I never tried it.'

' Well, I *have*,' said the old lady. ' When

I first retired from the educational pro-
fession I had no proper pride ; exacting
parents and their audacious offspring had
broken my spirit. I only wished to be
quiet and comfortable, and to this end—
among other things—I thought I would
furnish my sitting in church with a cushion
and a hassock. The next Sunday, when
I entered my pew, I found them both
occupied by another lady—mine was the
very first seat as you entered—and nothing
left for me but the bare seat and floor as
usual. I said nothing on that occasion.'

' Very foolish,' interposed Mr. Roden.

' But I could not make a disturbance
with a stranger in the sacred edifice.'

' Pardon me, my dear madam, it was
the very place for it; she would have been
more frightened than even you were, and
have given everything up at once.'

' At that time, however,' continued the
old lady, ' I had not your keen sense and
knowledge of the world. On the next

Sunday, however, when I again found the interloper in possession, I did venture to murmur, "I think, madam, this is my place;" and—would you believe it?—she said simply, " Oh, indeed!" and pushing *my* cushion, and *my* hassock up to the other end of the pew, left me the bare boards and the floor, just as before.'

' Exactly what I should have expected, and precisely what you deserved,' said Mr. Roden.

' Indeed, I think you are very hard on Nannie,' said Clare, smiling. ' What on earth could she have done under such circumstances ?'

' Why, my dear Clare, she could have sent for the beadle and got the woman turned out of the pew.'

' Well, to confess the truth, that is just what I did do,' said Miss Darrell naïvely. ' What are you all laughing at ? Was I not quite right, Mr. Oldcastle ?'

' No doubt you were quite right, madam ;

only, as an example of [passive obedience
carried out to the bitter end, the narrative
seems a little defective.'

'Well, at all events I am wiser now,'
insisted the quondam martyr ; 'and I only
wish,' she added, with a glance at Clare,
'I could impart my experience to others
who have a natural tendency to be trodden
on, but, unlike the worm, are averse to
turning.'

Clare only laughed good-naturedly.
They were walking (in complete privacy)
in the public garden, and all the sights and
sounds about them were redolent of the
beauty of the spring. The fresh air and
friendly companionship had done her good.
For the next few hours at all events she
would keep her mind free from troubles,
and not mar by downcast looks the enjoyment of those about her, two of whom, at
least, were putting themselves to inconvenience on her account. The despatch of
Mr. Oldcastle's letter had been a relief to

her, as any kind of action always is in such cases; and in particular his having informed Gerald that his silence or absence would be held equivalent to retractation gave her comfort. As a matter of fact, of course, Gerald could neither have written nor come to Sandford since the letter was sent; but in the meanwhile the truce suggested peace.

'Talking of being trodden on,' continued Miss Darrell, who was in high good-humour, and because Clare made no attempt at self-defence, imagined, perhaps, that she was on the road to conviction, ' I never knew what real oppression was till I flattered myself I was emancipated from it, and set up a page. The humiliation I have suffered through that boy exceeds all I have undergone from my one hundred and fifty young ladies. He leaves my most important morning callers behind the glass doors in the hall, for fear they should steal the umbrellas and things, and ushers all the begging-letter impostors up into the drawing-room; while out of doors he is worse than at home. When I go to pay visits in my hired brougham to the parents of my old pupils, and wish to be particularly dignified, he has to call in the assistance of the passers-by to reach the knockers ; and when I come out, instead of finding him at the carriage-door, I discover, to the ill-concealed delight of the powdered footman, that he is in the next street looking at Punch. He is always just where he ought not to be, and never where he ought to be.'

'He is here, at all events, looking for his mistress,' observed Mr. Roden, who had his eyeglass up, as was his habit when amused.

'Here! Where?' exclaimed the old lady, in extreme dismay. 'I left him on board wages.'

'It is the boy from the hotel,' observed Herbert quietly. 'He has a telegram.'

The message was for Mr. Oldcastle,

and, as all rightly concluded, from Gerald.

'I have nothing to retract of what I have said. It is all quite true. I cannot come to Sandford ; the whole subject is much too painful to me to bear discussion.'

The little party looked at one another in amazement.

'Well, upon my word, that *is* cool !' exclaimed Miss Darrell indignantly.

'Still it is very delicately expressed,' observed Mr. Roden in his blandest tones. 'I like the phrase "too painful." It shows a sensitive disposition.'

'Oh, Uncle Roden, don't laugh at it !' pleaded Clare pitifully ; 'it is such dreadful news.'

'Pardon me, my dear ; if you refer to the character of the writer, of which this message is certainly very significant, it is hardly to be called news. If you expected him to come here and submit himself to

cross-examination, you must have been
sanguine indeed.'

'What Miss Clare means is his sticking
to his story,' remarked the lawyer, 'which
is a serious matter.'

'Of course he sticks to it,' returned Mr.
Roden airily. 'When I was at Eton we
had an eleventh commandment, which we
broke less often than the others. "Tell a
lie, tell a good one, and stick to it;" in
spirit, at all events, this young gentleman
is an Etonian.'

'Nevertheless, it is evident to me,' said
Mr. Oldcastle thoughtfully, 'that whatever
may be his motive he means mischief. It
is impossible for us to ignore such a statement as he has committed himself to.'

'I should treat his story precisely as I
treat that slug yonder,' observed Mr. Roden,
pointing out the object in question with
the neatest of umbrellas. 'I should let it
alone.'

'Wherever it crawls it leaves a slime,'

answered the lawyer sententiously. 'In the slug's case it doesn't matter, but something must be done to stop *this*'—and he struck his hand upon the telegram, which he had spread out on his knee. 'If this sort of thing goes on, it will worry Miss Clare to fiddle-strings.'

'I would rather die than endure it,' said Clare firmly.

'Then we must produce counter-evidence—or rather, let us hope there will be no necessity to produce it; if we can only make sure of having it—to use if we want it—that will nip the mischief in the bud and frighten Gerald into veracity. What I now propose is to write to the only other person who was present at Oak Lodge on the night when Mr. Lyster died—Mr. Percy Fibbert.'

Mr. Roden uttered a little sniff of contempt; Miss Darrell pressed her lips together; Clare, pale as a ghost, cast down her eyes, which fell upon the lawyer's late metaphor, the slug, and shuddered.

'If something must be done,' said Herbert, 'I agree with Mr. Oldcastle that it must be that. We shall, after all, be asking no favour of him, but only that he shall speak the truth.'

'A difficult thing with some people when it is opposed to their interests,' remarked Mr. Roden drily. 'What do you say, Miss Darrell?'

'An impossible thing.'

'Still,' urged the lawyer, 'we shall be in no worse position than if Gerald goes to Percy, or it may be to Sir Peter himself, as I am inclined to think is more than possible.'

'Possible!' ejaculated Mr. Roden scornfully, 'it is certain; the whole affair is a plant between them from first to last.'

Miss Darrell cast a glance of admiration at the speaker which would have flattered Solomon. All she said was 'Ah!' but the interjection had the significance of a folio.

'Well, in that case,' pursued the lawyer, 'the affair might present itself in the form of a distinct claim. My suggestion is to anticipate and thereby prevent that. I propose to write in general terms to Mr. Percy Fibbert, admitting that a question had arisen as to the precise time at which Mr. Lyster expired, and recalling to his recollection the fact that the town clock struck twelve while he was at supper with Herbert and Miss Clare. All that I shall ask of him is a corroboration of that circumstance.'

'And suppose he declines to give it?' inquired Mr. Roden.

'Well, that will look ugly for him in the eyes of a jury—nay, my dear young lady,' for Clare had been about to make objections, 'I am quite aware that the case is never to come into court, but Mr. Percy Fibbert does not know that. He will take a practical view of the matter. If he answers truly, that will cut the ground away from Gerald's feet. You may say, indeed, that it will still be open to Gerald to repeat is statement; but upon the supposition that it is false he will forbear to do so, since nothing can then be got by it. Even you, my dear Miss Clare, will hardly, I conclude, give up your property on the unsupported word of this young man when it is also contradicted by independent testimony.'

'It is a frightful thing to entertain a doubt on such a matter,' said Clare hesitatingly. 'However slight it may be, it seems to me that Sir Peter—that is to say the firm—ought in honour to have the benefit of it.'

'My dear Clare,' interposed Mr. Roden, 'you are wearing my watch.'

'Your watch?'

'Yes; you may have had a conviction it was yours, but I have an idea that it's mine.

My idea may not be so strong as your conviction, but it creates a doubt ; and however slight that doubt may be, you are bound in honour to give it me.'

' My dear Uncle Roden,' said Clare, with a faint smile, ' the cases are not parallel. You have a watch of your own.'

' That is just what completes the parallel ; I have apparently no motive for depriving you of your watch, just as Gerald to our eyes has no motive. But that does not make either of our claims less preposterous. Do, I beseech you, behave like a reasonable being.'

If Miss Darrell had known Mr. Roden better, she would have admired him even more than she did for the attitude he had assumed with respect to Gerald and his story. During the whole of his existence he had probably never taken so much trouble, or interested himself half so much in the affairs of a fellow-creature. But in addition to his liking for Clare, and his detestation of the Fibberts (whom he really believed to be at the bottom of it all), he resented beyond measure the possibility of his niece giving way to her morbid and Quixotic feelings in the matter. As an heiress, she reflected credit on him ; but should she be mad enough to strip herself of her fortune through these foolish scruples, she would be a credit to nobody, and, if he had been of a weaker disposition, might even become a burthen to him. For all she knew (though *he* knew better) he *was* wealthy; and her conduct aggravated him all the more, since it seemed to him that she was ready to make a sacrifice at his expense, the very wickedest thing in his eyes that any human being could propose to himself.

' If you have any regard for your friends, Clare,' pleaded Miss Darrell, unconsciously following up this argument, ' I entreat you to follow their advice in a matter so momentous.'

Thus pressed on all sides, Clare cast an appealing glance at Herbert.

'I used to think it was always easy to know what was right,' she sighed, 'but now it seems so difficult; what would you do, Herbert, if you were in my place?'

'I should put myself in the hands of a just man, who also knew the ways of the unjust,' replied Herbert with an inclination of his head towards Mr. Oldcastle.

'Then be so good, my dear Mr. Oldcastle,' said Clare firmly, 'as to write that letter to—' her lips quivered, as though declining to pronounce Percy's name— 'the letter, that is, which you have suggested.'

Mr. Roden looked thunders, and frowned so hard that his glass fell out of his eye, and Miss Darrell lifted her hands from her lap in silent protest; but Mr. Oldcastle bowed like a lawyer who has received his instructions, and to whom it only remains to carry them out.

CHAPTER XXXIV

CHIVALRY.

BY common consent, and also because opinion was so divided among the little party, the subject of Gerald was dropped for the remainder of the day. The lawyer's letter was despatched in due course to Percy's address in London, and for the present there was an end of the matter. Mr. Roden withdrew himself in dudgeon from the rest of the party until dinner-time, and gave himself up to his own devices. With his gold eyeglass and superior bearing he patronised Sandford to that extent that if patronage could have done it, independent of numbers, the

dreams of the Railway Company in creating the place would have been realised—
its fortunes would have been made. As
it was, he rather impoverished them; for
finding in the guide-book that the lift used
many thousand gallons of water in its
ascent and only cost a penny to the hirer,
including the services of an attendant, he
amused himself by going up and down in
it, taking especial care to use it when nobody else desired its accommodation. By
this invigorating exercise and the consciousness that he had got his money's worth out
of it and more, Mr. Roden so far worked
off his ill-humour as to meet the lawyer
(who was the chief cause of it) at the
dinner-table with renewed complacency;
but when the ladies retired for the night
he also lit his bed-candle, and took his
cigarette with him to his bedroom in
preference to remaining with the other
two.

Thus, for the first time since they came

to Sandford, Mr. Oldcastle and Herbert found themselves alone together.

'Now that that cantankerous gentleman has taken himself off, my lad,' said the lawyer, as soon as the door had closed behind their late companion, 'I should like to have a few words with you. A second consultation of five, and two of them ladies, is not a thing I have a taste for ; and I doubt if the result of the first will be satisfactory.'

'Still I think we have done—or rather you have done—the best that could be done under the circumstances.'

'Let us hope so ; but to tell you the truth, I am much more apprehensive about what may come of the affair than I have cared to show. I have reason to entertain a very bad opinion of Master Gerald Lyster. Clare has often assured me that the young gentleman is nobody's enemy but his own ; but that is sometimes a very dangerous sort of person, eh ?'

The lawyer's tone was interrogative ; he seemed to expect some revelation from his companion that might throw further light on Gerald's character : but Herbert only answered gravely, ' That is so, no doubt.'

' I know, of course, that he is a very young fellow, but still there are sad stories about him ; a man in my position in a place like Stokeville hears a good deal about people.'

' Naturally.'

' Now I don't want you to tell tales out of school, Herbert, but it is important that I should thoroughly understand our posi- tion, which is affected by his own. The time, too, has quite gone by for any false delicacy, or reticence, as regards this fellow. Is Gerald married ?'

' I don't know. I have heard it stated that he is, but I have never believed it.'

' That is, from what you know of his character, you think he is much too selfish to have sacrificed his prospects, as his father did, from any scruples of morality. But it may be, as he would put it, that he couldn't help himself. He has certainly something on his mind which troubles him; he is always in urgent need of money; girls of his own rank in life seem to have no attractions for him. Upon the whole, it is my impression that he *is* married.'

'It is quite possible.'

'In that case there may be motives for his present proceeding; for that his whole story is a lie, I take it for granted you are convinced. It is so, is it not?'

'It is, I am quite sure, an invention from beginning to end,' said Herbert.

'Just so. Well, if he's married, there may have been many things to quicken his invention—necessities.'

Herbert shook his head.

'Ah, but you don't know. His wife is, I hear, expecting a son and heir; and he has debts besides. These things make a man look about him. He must have funds from somebody. Gerald invents this tale, to get them out of his half-sister in the shape of hush-money.'

'Gerald never invented it,' said Herbert quietly.

'What do you mean? You surely don't agree with Mr. Roden that the whole affair is got up between him and the Fibberts to deprive Clare of her share in the profits of the firm. He called it "a plant." It made my blood run cold to hear him. Why, Sir Peter, with all his faults, would sooner see his museum burnt down than do such a thing.'

'I don't deny it; I don't wish to say a word against Sir Peter nor anyone else. But I am quite sure that Gerald did not originate this scheme.'

'You mean he is not an inventor like yourself; hasn't got the wits for it? But perhaps some of his belongings have. There's that Sam Chigwell, for instance, a very cunning fellow, who, moreover, as

I have reason to believe, has already been mixed up discreditably with Gerald's affairs. If it be so, it may prove very difficult to keep matters quiet, as Clare has set her heart upon doing. Though, on the other hand Percy's answer to our letter should be final. When Gerald hears we have got that, he will know that the game is up.'

'Do you build very much on Percy's reply?'

'Most certainly I do. With Clare in this Quixotic and morbid state of mind, which of course ties our hands, what else have we to build upon? The whole edifice of our defence rests upon it: as to our legal rights, those could be established easily enough, I flatter myself, in any court in England; but there's Clare. Her scruples stand in our way. Now, with Percy's word to back us——'

'You will never get it,' interrupted Herbert; 'that, at least, is my firm conviction.'

'What? Why, you yourself advocated my writing to him !'

'Because it was the only chance which suggested itself in Clare's favour ; the only plan which, if successful, would satisfy her. I may be wrong, but I fear it will not be successful.'

'My dear Herbert, you astound me ! Do you think, then, with Mr. Roden, that Percy is a scoundrel? You must surely have some reason besides personal dislike (for I know, of course, you dislike him) for imputing to him such a course of conduct.'

Herbert flushed to the temples. 'You will please to remember, Mr. Oldcastle, that I have volunteered no expression of opinion regarding Mr. Percy Fibbert, whom, as you justly observe, I do not like. But we are discussing Clare's affairs, and since you tell me they depend on Percy's aid, I must needs say that I believe it will be withheld. What you wish him to do is, in effect, to cancel his own claim to

Clare's profits in the firm for the year, as also his uncle's claim. On the latter ground he may reasonably decline to assist us.'

' Even by telling the truth?'

' If you put it that way I answer, "Yes."'

' Unless you know something of Percy Fibbert which I don't know, I think, Herbert, you are very uncharitable. It is possible he may have behaved ill to Clare— it is that, is it? You didn't say so—no ; but I can see what has prejudiced you against him. Well, I can only say that I think your suspicions unworthy of you.'

' I am very sorry, Mr. Oldcastle. But after all, since in twenty-four hours we shall see which of us is right, it is hardly worth while to discuss the matter.'

The lawyer rose from his chair and began to pace the room uneasily.

' If you had said " Percy Fibbert is a thief," or " Percy Fibbert is capable of forgery," you could hardly have astonished me more, Herbert. I feel sure you are

mistaken, my dear lad. But if you are not
—I have not told Clare, because I thought
it would be injudicious; since the greater
disadvantage to herself the more she would
be set on doing what she calls justice to her
father's memory—but if Percy does play us
false, so far as Clare is concerned; this may
mean ruin.'

' Ruin ?'

' Yes, nothing less; that Bank in which
her father was so mad as to invest his
money, turned out even worse than I expected—much worse. I trusted to the
profits of the firm for the year to make her
straight; but if she doesn't get them, her
whole fortune—that is, all she has invested
in the concern—will hardly meet her liabilities.'

' Good heavens !'

' It is perfectly true. Roden showed his
sense—confound him !—in washing his
hands of all responsibility. And that reminds me, by-the-bye, that although he has

done so, he may, as Clare's nominal trustee, make himself obnoxious to yourself.'

' To me ? How is that possible ?'

' Well, in this way ; of course one hopes it may never happen ; but if Gerald sticks to his story, and Percy shows any disposition to side with him—if anything, in fact, in the shape of a claim is set up to Clare's beneficial interest in the firm, she will give up everything at once.   From that, no argument, I am convinced, will turn her. She will throw everything overboard rather than the least stigma should attach to her father's memory.'

' That is certain,' said Herbert.

' Very good ; in that case, when her liabilities with respect to the Bank have been settled, there will, as I have said, be very little left of the principal invested in the firm ; a few thousand pounds at most will be all she will then have to live upon. But what Roden will say, or may say, is this : " Mr. Lyster had thirty thousand pounds in the business; you tell me ten thousand pounds of it is Herbert Newton's, but where is the proof of that?" And, indeed, thanks to your own dilatoriness in the matter, there is no proof. Of course it will make no difference to you, because Clare would rather cut her right hand off than take advantage of such a circumstance; but I do think it quite possible that Roden, who as one can see is horrified at the idea of anyone belonging to him becoming poor, may make himself unpleasant about it. I may say that Mr. Lyster's conduct in the matter was something worse than the sin of omission; I don't mean to say that he wilfully took advantage of your characteristic carelessness as to money matters to leave the thing in doubt; but to have left behind him no legal acknowledgment of your rights, and not even to have explained to you the circumstances——'

'My dear Mr. Oldcastle,' interrupted

the young man earnestly, 'you are labouring under the strangest mistake, and it is only due to my poor uncle to enlighten you. Before his death, so far from making no allusion to it, he and I came to a complete understanding in the matter. Our conversation was of a private nature, but I may state this much, without breach of confidence, that my ten thousand pounds in Fibbert and Lyster's business is, in fact, only mine provisionally.'

'Provisionally. How can that be? It was your own money, which you inherited when you came of age, and which Mr. Lyster invested for you in the concern; and a very good per cent. it paid at that time, though it fell off afterwards before this great spurt came.'

'That is very true; but the arrangement I speak off was long subsequent. May I speak to you as a client—I mean, will you hold the communication sacred as to privacy?'

'Of course I will.'

'Do you remember a letter left by Mr. Lyster addressed to me, but only to be delivered in case he died before the 1st of January?'

'I do. It was destroyed unopened, according to his instructions.'

'Well, if it had not been destroyed you would have learnt from it what I am now about to tell you. He had very grave apprehensions about those unhappy bank shares, which it seems have been partly realised.'

'They might have ruined him, stock, lock, and barrel,' observed the lawyer sententiously.

'No doubt they might; he had a dreadful suspicion they would. If he had died before the 1st of January, and Clare had not inherited her interest in the firm for the present year—which, observe, is exactly the position in which she will be placed if she gives credence to Gerald's story—he thought it possible that his liabilities might

swallow up her whole fortune, which, since
as you say I had no legal acknowledgment
of my claim, would have included mine as
well.'

'A most abominable and shameful risk
to run,' observed the lawyer indignantly.

'But not so, if it was done with my own
knowledge and approval.'

Mr. Oldcastle gazed at the young man
with a sort of sublime admiration.

'In that case it would be—legally—
justifiable.   But as to morals—'

'Nay, that is not *your* business,' returned
the young man naïvely.   'There was, as
you say, a risk, but that I acceded to ; nay,
more, if you will have it so, there was an
intentional wrong, but that I forgave him.
It was thoroughly understood between the
dying man and me that if that money was
lost I should rub it off like a bad debt and
say nothing about it.'

'Say nothing about it,' echoed the lawyer, rubbing his chin as if to arouse him-

self from a dream, if dream it was; 'say nothing about ten thousand pounds?'

'Now, as it happens,' continued the young man, 'it is very possible—in my opinion almost certain—that Mr. Lyster's estate will be placed in the precise position which he apprehended.'

'But not by the same means,' remarked Mr. Oldcastle.

'Quite true; but, so far as I am concerned, the agreement which I entered into is equally binding.'

The lawyer shook his head.

'What?' cried Herbert contemptuously. 'Am I to receive the thanks of a dying man, the gratitude for what he chose to consider a great service—but which, in my opinion, was only a part payment for the kindness and affectionate consideration always displayed to me by him and his— and then to cry off the bargain and keep my money? Would you have me be as base as Gerald?'

' No, Herbert, you are not base—certainly
not base,' said Mr. Oldcastle, laying his
hand upon the other's shoulder ; 'but there
is such a thing (though it's not very fre-
quent) as going too far in the other
direction.   Now, though a lawyer, I am
an honest man, and I cannot consent to be
a party to such a self-sacrifice.'

' The duty of an honest lawyer, Mr.
Oldcastle, is surely owed in the first place
to his client.   I tell you this money is not
mine ; it is surely not your place, as Clare's
legal adviser, to question her right to it.
If you did so, though it would be most
distressing to me to have to do so, I
should appeal from your judgment to
that of your co-trustee, Mr. Roden, who,
I am sure, would take my view of the
matter.'

' I don't doubt it,' said the lawyer, smiling.
' But even if it should be so, or if I myself
could be persuaded to take advantage of
your generosity in this matter, there is one

person whose consent would never be given to such a proposal—namely, Clare herself.'

'Clare's consent must never be asked,' answered Herbert vehemently. ' You have given your word to me to keep secret what has passed between us.'

'But she will naturally say to me, " Where does this money come from ? How is it that I have thirty thousand pounds instead of twenty, wherewith to settle these liabilities?" '

' She will do nothing of the kind; you know as well as I do, Mr. Oldcastle, that her indifference to money matters is almost equalled by her ignorance of them. Whatever you choose to tell her she will believe —or rather, on whatever point you choose to be reticent she will ask no questions. Her own property may be more, or her debt to the Bank may be less—what does it matter ? She will only look to the total.'

'Upon my life, sir, you are very ingenious; if you took to cheating other people besides yourself you might become dangerous. But at present you are new to knavery. It is necessary before the commission of a pecuniary fraud to look at the matter all round. Now Miss Clare, although as you say indifferent enough to her own affairs, takes a great interest in those of her friends. She may, I admit, be inclined to take for granted that you have received your ten thousand pounds, but she will very soon remark that you are not living upon it—that, in fact, you have nothing to live upon.'

'Oh, that's all right,' said Herbert lightly; 'I had stupidly forgotten to say what, if I had mentioned it at first, would have spared you all astonishment. I am now, thanks to the liberality of the Railway Company, quite independent. A suggestion as to the economy of fuel, arising curiously enough out of my own diving experiment—

I'll tell you all about it some day—has been favourably received, and is, in fact, adopted. I am in receipt of a good income.'

' What do you call a good income ?'

' Whatever is sufficient to its possessor. I tell you I have lots of money, and how is Clare to know where it comes from ? If I don't seem to live extravagantly, so much the better; she will give me credit for prudence.'

' But what will the world say ?'

' That is a matter of absolute indifference to me. Perhaps I shall be represented as hoarding treasure, and become greatly respected. At all events I am quite fixed as to what ought to be done, and must be done.'

' You are as Quixotic as Clare herself,' said Mr. Oldcastle. ' I could not bring myself to say " yes" to such a proposal as you have just made, but that I feel sure there will be no occasion to put it into effect. To-morrow evening's post will, I am convinced, bring a letter from Percy, which will put an end to our troubles.'

' If it does, I shall be as pleased as yourself,' said Herbert, smiling, 'and at the same time shall have gained a character from you for self-sacrifice at the cheapest possible rate. You know I am an early riser, so I will wish you good-night.'

Mr. Oldcastle shook the young man's hand as though he would never let go of it.

' This beats me altogether,' mused the lawyer, as he nursed his leg before the fire. ' There is no precedent for it in the books. If this Herbert Newton were an older man—that is, a good deal older—I should have said he must have been some offspring of Adam before the Fall.'

END OF VOL. II.

BILLING AND SONS, PRINTERS AND ELECTROTYPERS, GUILDFORD.

www.ingramcontent.com/pod-product-compliance
Lightning Source LLC
Chambersburg PA
CBHW060525030726
47498CB00004B/1081